More Books by Rabia Gale

The Reflected City
Ghostlight

The Sunless World
Quartz
Flare
Flux

Taurin's Chosen
Mourning Cloak
Ironhand

Rainbird

Ghostlight

The Reflected City Book One

Rabia Gale

RABIA GALE
FANTASY AUTHOR

Happy
reading!

R. Gale

Ghostlight

Published by Rabia Gale
www.rabiagale.com
Cover design by Deranged Doctor Design

ISBN-13: 978-1727189605
ISBN-10: 1727189604

Ghostlight

The Reflected City Book One

To my husband, for his support, and to my children, who keep life entertaining.

Chapter One

TREVELYAN SHIELD KNEW ARABELLA TRENT was trouble the moment he laid eyes on her that spring morning.

He was a trifle foxed, staggering home from the Plush Purple Peacock through streets filled with a pale golden haze. A happy fog occupied most, but not all, of his head. He could never quite turn off the watchful part that was currently keeping him from embracing a street lamp and attempting to waltz with it. Trey couldn't quite understand why, but he was sure he'd be grateful for it later.

In the meantime, he had to navigate the early morning rush, a task that was more than usually difficult today.

Carts laden with milk and eggs trundled past him, pulled by dray horses who showed their pegasus heritage in vestigial wings and feathered hoofs. Their drivers shouted and cursed as the traffic inevitably snarled. Housewives on their way to market hurried down the footpath, jostling passersby with their large baskets. The pungent smells of spoiled milk and horse dung hung in the air.

All Trey wanted was his bed so he could block out the entirety of Lumen for a few blissful hours. A few hours to forget his life and his work, the dull heartache that still hadn't eased, and the weight of the viscount's title that he had never wanted.

And then he saw her.

Arabella Trent hesitated at the corner of Chipping Hill and Holgate, plainly waiting for an opening in the traffic. She wore a shrine cloak of traditional grey, its hood slipping off her head to reveal a riot of dark curls.

But it wasn't the cloak that caught Trey's attention, nor the curls. Neither did her large, lustrous eyes, nor her dainty nose, nor her slender figure—nor, indeed, any of the other considerable charms that Miss Trent possessed.

Rather, he was arrested by the way the sunlight shone through her translucent form.

Trey closed his eyes and counted to ten. Surely the apparition was a figment concocted by his exhausted mind and an excess of the Peacock's excellent brandy. When he opened his eyes, she'd be gone.

He cracked an eyelid.

She was still there.

Trey considered a strategic retreat. He'd go home, send a message to the Office about the spirit, *then* fall face forward onto his bed.

After all, he had just spent half the night exorcising a particularly pernicious haunt. Dealing kindly and gently with a debutante was a trying exercise for him at the best of times. In his current state, it would be nigh on impossible.

The ghost of Arabella Trent turned and saw him. Pleased recognition lit up her eyes. She tilted her head at him in a way that invited, if not outright commanded, his help.

Trey struggled briefly with himself. Generations of good breeding won over selfish desire. With a mental farewell to his bed, which had retreated further and further away from him, he crossed the street to the young woman.

Her aethereal substance, he noted, gleamed with the luster of a pearl.

A relieved smile spread across Miss Trent's face as he approached. "Lord St. Ash," she greeted him with the title that still didn't fit, "good morning."

She had to have dimples, thought Trey darkly. Charming ones.

Miss Trent faltered at his expression. Trey knew just how forbidding it was, having cultivated it in front of his mirror as a boy.

"Miss Trent," he said without preamble, "what are you doing here all by yourself?"

She looked stricken. Trey winced. He had just accused her of gross impropriety.

He was no good with very young women like her, dead or alive. He had never bothered to temper his blunt speech or aloof demeanor around them. At least he had never made Miss Trent cry. Not to his recollection, anyway. Still it'd be best to fetch Hilda who was far better at this…

The realization hit him like a bucketful of cold water, washing away the last mists of inebriation, leaving only a throbbing ache. Hilda wasn't here anymore. Nor were so many of the other phantasmists. Not after the Incursion.

He had to do this on his own.

Miss Trent's hands fluttered as she explained. "Oh! Of course I wasn't here by myself. My friends and I formed a party to visit Shrine Park at dawn." She gestured at the screen of yews behind her. "Somehow I was separated from them, and now I cannot seem to cross this street at all. I'm so glad you came, my lord! I was beginning to think I had turned completely invisible."

You have. Trey bit down on the words, unable to say them with Miss Trent's eyes meeting his with frank amusement.

Instead he looked over her shoulder to where Shrine Park brooded behind its barrier of evergreens and stone walls. The massive wrought-iron gates warned away rather than welcomed in. It was like another world in there, quiet and weighty, cut off from the life of the city. Had this young woman died there? He found that hard to believe, not with the monastic orders keeping watch over the place.

"I didn't know people still visited shrines during the Vernal Rites," he remarked. High society was generally glad to leave religious obligations for Holy Week, which would begin in three days. "I thought it had fallen out of fashion."

"Well, I am decidedly *unfashionable*." Even as a ghost, Miss Trent was more animated than most people managed while being alive. Her eyes fairly danced with enthusiasm. "I came to Lumen late last autumn, and I want to see and do *everything*, no matter how rustic people think me. My friends were kind enough to indulge me by visiting the shrines today, but I have stupidly misplaced them and caused them trouble." Faint frown lines appeared between her brows, a detail that wasn't lost on Trey.

She must be very recently dead.

He was starting to feel sorry for her. It was a dangerous emotion, especially in his occupation. Apparitions often transformed from piteous victims to murderous specters with alarming rapidity.

But since this oblivious ghost showed no signs of growing fangs and attacking him, he merely said, "Then let me take you home, before your guardians are needlessly worried about you. You live with the Elliots, do you not?"

"Yes. Aunt Cecilia is my father's sister. We reside on Crescent Circle, in Bottleham."

"Come, then." Trey caught the eye of an oncoming carter, gestured imperiously, and strode into the road. With a baleful glare, the driver reined in his horse. Behind him, other carters halted their own vehicles, cries of "Make way for the gentleman!" going down the whole line.

Miss Trent squeaked, gathered up her cloak and white skirt, and scurried after him. Her incorporeal feet made no sound on the dusty street, but she didn't appear to notice.

She gave him an appreciative look as they stepped once more onto pavement. "Well done!"

"For managing to cross the road without being flattened? I thank you," said Trey dryly.

His tone did nothing to dampen her merriment. "When I made the attempt, I was attacked by geese and almost run over. That is why I'm so impressed."

Trey was tempted to explain that almost being run over was the least of Miss Trent's troubles. But he settled for, "No geese in sight. You're safe, Miss Trent."

"Indeed." She matched his longer strides with quick ones of her own, not complaining at the pace he set. "I can see you are one of those competent and useful sort of men. I'm glad you came along!"

Trey wasn't. A headache pounded in his temples. However, he could hardly tell Miss Trent that he was contemplating the least bothersome way to send her off into her afterlife.

Pedestrian traffic gave way before Trey the same way the carters had. Maybe it was his air of unconscious authority or the hum of magic that surrounded him.

Or perhaps it was that he projected a formidable vexation.

Whatever the reason, the flow of laborers and housewives parted around him, giving him wider berth than was strictly necessary. Trey considered this to be for Miss Trent's benefit— even an oblivious ghost like her could hardly fail to notice if she walked through a basket of mackerel. She certainly wouldn't appreciate a close encounter with the fish's silver scales and round eyes.

They proceeded in silence for a while as the crowds thinned out around them, before Miss Trent spoke again. "To be candid," she confided, "I had always thought you a trifle aloof."

"I thought you were being candid," remarked Trey. "I think the word you're looking for is disagreeable. Or maybe toplofty. Haughty?" He examined the pale sky above some chimney pots, weighing the word. "Yes, haughty would definitely do."

"If you say so, my lord." Dimples peeped in her cheeks again. Her hood had slipped off her glossy head, so he could clearly make out her expression with a quick glance. "I recall you displayed a lack of enthusiasm when you danced with me at the Holmsteads' two weeks ago."

"It was in self-defense."

"From me?" Her brow furrowed.

"No." He gave her a sideways look and grinned. "I have been battling all of society's matrons for years. You were unfortunately caught in the crossfire."

"Oh?" She looked intrigued and amused. "What is the nature of this conflict, my lord?"

Trey shrugged. "It is simply that I am young, unattached, and of good birth. It is my duty, according to society, to be available to even out numbers at a supper party or make a fourth at cards."

"Or partner a lady who would otherwise have to sit out a dance," Miss Trent put in. She sidled past two barrels some chandler had seen fit to place outside his shop. The stench of tallow filled the air.

"Precisely." Trey's lips twisted in a self-mocking smile. "I admit I have little use for social niceties, so I do my best to discourage hostesses from thinking of me when making up their guest lists. But perhaps I should not have told you."

"I'll take your secret to the grave," she vowed in mock-seriousness.

A chill went over Trey. Out of habit, the fingers of his left hand curled, seeking a sword hilt.

Miss Trent gave him a slight, puzzled frown. She went on, less brightly, "For an instant back at the park, I was afraid you would turn on your heel and leave me to my fate on the street corner."

"I almost did." His own honesty startled him. Was it Miss Trent herself who invited confidences, or her circumstances? After all, as a ghost she no longer counted as a member of the polite society Trey kept at arm's length. He pushed on. "So you see, Miss Trent, your first impression of me was the correct one. I am quite disagreeable."

She didn't answer. Glancing down at her, Trey saw a look of serious sympathy on her face. The expression sent a frisson of recognition through him, though he couldn't remember why.

"It gets lonely, doesn't it," she said softly, "holding the world at a distance?"

Before he could respond, Miss Trent's attention shifted. With a muffled exclamation, she darted ahead to where a cart stood in the street, surrounded by interested onlookers. "Stop it! Stop mistreating that unfortunate child *at once*."

She hurried past the spectators, not noticing how the large right sleeve of her cloak dragged through the arm of a small man in a leather apron.

The brutish man in work-stained clothes did not, in fact, refrain from cuffing the cringing boy he held by one ear. Miss Trent's vehemence was entirely wasted on him. Trey thought he'd better intervene before her wrath turned her into some grey-skinned hag with bat wings.

"You there!" Trey hailed the man. "What are you doing to that unfortunate child—I mean, that boy?"

The man craned his head towards Trey in bug-eyed surprise. "'E's a thief, mister," he said self-righteously. "Snatched an apple off

7

me cart. I's got to disc'pline 'im, see. Right useless piece of work, 'e is." He shook the unlovely child who howled something to the effect that Tommy made him do it, it wasn't his fault, and other details Trey had no interest in pursuing.

"Discipline!" exclaimed Miss Trent, flushed with indignation and still showing no signs of growing fangs. "That's not discipline; it's just taking his own nasty temper out on the boy!"

"Put the boy down, man. I can hardly hear myself think above his yowling." Pain throbbed behind Trey's eyes. He glared at the gathered onlookers and asked in a glacial tone, "Don't you people have somewhere else to be?" At which point, they remembered several pressing appointments and dispersed, some in haste, others reluctantly.

The carter released his captive, who looked as if he would take to his heels. Trey prevented this by putting a hand on the urchin's thin shoulder. The boy's sharp-featured face was pinched under the grime.

"Hungry, are you?" he asked.

A wary look crept into the urchin's eyes. His gaze flicked from Trey's face to focus on something beyond his shoulder—

He was looking at Miss Trent. He could *see* her. Trey's hand tightened and the boy yelped.

"Answer the gent, you!" The carter raised his hand to smack the boy, only to be stopped short by Trey's cold glare.

"Yes! I'm 'ungry, sir," said the thief in a rush. "'Twas only one apple, sir, and 'alf-rotted, too."

"Now look 'ere," roared the carter, anger suffusing his face at these aspersions cast on his fruit.

"How much?" snapped Trey.

"Beg pardon, sir?"

"Never mind," muttered Trey. He fished in his pocket and came up with a copper coin. He tossed it at the carter. "Take this for your trouble. I'll deal with the boy."

The carter stared, first at Trey, then at the coin. Then he shrugged, as if washing his hands off the whole business and turned to his cart.

"My lord," Miss Trent broke in, "I think we ought to—"

"Just a moment, Miss Trent!" said Trey. "I believe I've just volunteered to deal with this boy." *Just like I made you my problem*, he thought ruefully.

It must be the effects of the Peacock's brandy. He was normally not so quixotic.

Trey looked down at the urchin whose gaze was flickering back and forth between his two benefactors, eyes full of alarmed suspicion. "What's your name, boy?"

"Jem, sir." The boy straightened to attention.

"Well, Jem, I'm not in the habit of bailing out thieves, no matter what their age. But I'll give you a chance to earn your keep. Lying and stealing won't be tolerated, you will submit to a bath, and you'll have to work. But in return you'll get a warm place to sleep and food to fill your belly. What do you say? Be quick about it—I haven't the time."

Indecision warred in the boy's expression. Trey waited. Finally, the urchin took a deep breath and squared his shoulders. "Aye, sir. I'll do it."

"Good boy." Trey released his grip. "First thing, go to Hopechurch Street. You know where it is?" At the boy's nod, Trey took a piece of paper from his pocket. He brought it to life with a touch. A strand of aether, shimmering grey, coiled itself into a series of runes, sinking into the fibers. Trey folded the missive into a complex shape, pressed his thumb into the place where the folds met. A sizzle and the Shield insignia appeared in fiery colors, holding the message shut.

"Golly!" Jem's eyes went wide. Miss Trent, ghostly and glimmering and hovering a few inches off the pavement, looked on with interest.

"You know the Quadrangle?"

Jem blanched. "That place where they muck about with dead people and 'venging sp'rits and such?"

"That's the one." Trey's grin was malicious. "Take this message to a man named Morgan who works there. You'll have no trouble getting someone to point him out."

"What then?" The boy's expression was suspicious.

"Then you do as Morgan says. Congratulations, Jem. You are now a civil servant, the God-Father help us all."

"You didn' say that at first!" squawked the boy.

"Changing your mind?" Trey arched his eyebrows.

"'Course not. You said warm bed and full belly, right?" Jem snatched the message and stuffed it down his ragged shirt. "I'll be there." He glowered at Trey. "'Sides you got yer hands full 'ere, dontcha?" He ran off before Trey could say anything else.

Trey eyed the urchin's departing figure, wondering if he would regret this. Morgan would give him an earful, no doubt, for saddling him with the boy. But people who saw apparitions were rare to begin with. It wasn't every day you ran into a seer.

Boy disposed of, he turned to face his bigger problem.

Miss Trent favored him with a long-suffering look. "I was going to say," she remarked, "that Lady Holmstead's new orphan house might be a good place for Jem."

"Not for such a streetwise brat," Trey countered. "Believe me, Morgan will do Jem a sight more good than all of Lady Holmstead's matrons."

"And here I thought you agreed that her orphan house was a most noble endeavor. You listened to me prose on about it for fully a quarter of an hour at her supper!"

"Did I? I was probably thinking of something else." Trey resumed walking Crescent Circle-wards and Miss Trent fell in beside him. She didn't appear to notice—or mind if she had—that he hadn't offered her his arm.

"I hope you have also not forgotten your promise to donate a hundred pounds to the charity."

Trey frowned. "I have a vague recollection of vowing such a thing to stop the prosing."

Her dimples peeped again. "Yes, I do have a knack for acquiring large sums of money from our donors," she said complacently.

"What a conniving chit you are," Trey remarked without heat. "Was this your revenge for my lack of enthusiasm in dancing with you?"

"I would *never*." The twinkle in her eyes belied her statement.

Miss Trent kept up a bright stream of chatter, mostly centered around her delight at the spring festivities in Lumen, which culminated in the grand assembly at Merrimack's tomorrow night, followed by a procession to the Keep the morning after.

Trey listened in silence, partly because he didn't want to be seen talking to empty air and partly out of bemusement. Most of the apparitions he encountered were decidedly insane. They certainly didn't hold conversations about social events while he tried not to notice their long lashes or slender hands.

Miss Trent didn't attract the notice of any other seers, though he couldn't say the same for stray elementals. An undine rose from a muddy puddle to stare at the ghost out of silvered eyes. A flock of sylphs, mere diaphanous glimmers, darted above their heads before flying off to torment a sleeping tabby cat.

"And I have always wanted to see the Mirror of Elsinore up close," Miss Trent finished. The Mirror, the centerpiece of the Procession, was a national treasure guarded zealously by the government and removed from its hiding place only once a year.

"You can't," said Trey crushingly. "They call it the Viewing, but no one's allowed into the solar save for the Guardians. Revitalizing a priceless magical object that protects our borders is not a public spectacle."

"Another time then," said Miss Trent, uncrushed.

They were in Bottleham, a quiet genteel neighborhood of terraced houses in red brick rather than the white-washed stucco and grey stone of more modern architecture. A milkman's cart and horse rattled by, two maids beat rugs on a stair railing, and an elderly gentleman took the air, followed by his gnome servant. Trey received some curious looks; no one else appeared to notice Miss Trent.

"It's the house just up ahead, with the yellow door. Uncle Henry grumbles about the color, but I think it's sunny and cheerful." Miss Trent paused, her attention on the hackney pulled up to the house in question.

A tall, thin man, black bag in hand, sprang up the steps and was admitted inside.

"That's Dr. Barkley, my aunt's physician." Miss Trent's brows drew together.

A pair of girls, arms around each other, emerged from the house. Both looked pale and shaken, their heads bowed, not paying attention to anything else.

Which was good because Trey, with an inward sigh, recognized one of the two. Charlotte Blake—known to all her family as Charlie—was the younger sister of a college friend. The large, rambunctious Blake family had somewhat adopted him during those years; he'd spent many of his holidays in their rather ramshackle, but always lively, household.

And now he felt beholden to help the friend of a girl he fondly considered a younger sister.

"And those are my friends! Why, what has happened?" cried Miss Trent. She started forward, her feet rising a few inches from the ground.

"Miss Trent!" Trey added a compulsion to his command; Miss Trent turned to him, her feet settling back onto the ground.

"Is someone ill, my lord?" she whispered. In the stronger light, she looked more insubstantial than ever. "Or... or... is it...?"

Trey wished again he could hand this off to Hilda, who'd mothered everyone and had always known the right thing to say. But it was Trevelyan Shield who stood here now. He ran his hand through his already tousled hair. And it was still only Thursday.

Best get it over with.

"Miss Trent, raise your hand and look at it."

"What?" She stared at him as she lifted her arm. "What's wrong with—?"

Miss Trent glanced at her hand and froze. Her eyes grew wide. Her mouth rounded.

"You'll have to forgive me, Miss Trent. I'm not at all good at breaking things gently." Trey made a complicated gesture as she started to scream.

Miss Trent's form glowed blue, collapsed into itself, and winked out.

Trey stared at the Elliots' sunshine-yellow door.

It was, he knew, going to be another long day.

Chapter Two

ARABELLA TRENT WAS TRAPPED IN a pentagram five paces across from side to side.

She knew this because she had traversed its shape multiple times, testing the pentagram's strength. After being thrown back by the wards every single instance, she had to concede defeat.

Besides, the buzz of angry magic *hurt*.

Even though I'm a ghost, I can still feel pain.

The thought was like an open pit in a stomach she didn't have.

If she was a ghost, it meant that she—

—was dead.

"How can I be dead?" she demanded out loud to the empty chamber. "I don't even remember how I got this way. There must be some mistake."

No response.

A knot tightened in Arabella's middle. Dead or not, she couldn't *bear* being trapped. She had to get free.

Think.

She couldn't get through the wards. Could she perhaps get under or over them? But the stone floor below her feet refused to allow her incorporeal body passage. And she couldn't hover more than a few inches off the ground without being pressed back down as if by a giant's hands.

Perhaps she could shift the anchors of the pentagram and nullify the spell that way? Arabella examined the floor, but the lines had been scored into the stone and inlaid with gold. The pentagram was made to be permanent.

Whatever happened to using plain old chalk? Not that it would've helped her much. She couldn't affect the material world. Scuffing chalk lines was outside her scope.

Arabella paced her prison, hoping the exercise would either expose some weakness in the wards or dislodge a brilliant plan of escape from her stumped brain.

Neither occurred, but the activity did calm her down. Her fast, shallow breaths subsided—she wouldn't think about the fact that she was not actually respiring—and rationality asserted itself.

This isn't like those other times. It isn't pitch dark and close. I'm not restrained and I can still see.

Arabella circled her current domain a few more times, then gave up her attempts to secure her freedom. The sight of the ground gleaming through her translucent feet made her feel ill.

She flopped onto the floor and drew her knees up to her chest. With a kind of distant surprise, she noted her clothing had changed. Instead of the shrine cloak and white robes, she wore her new high-necked walking dress of sea green with four inches of silver embroidery at the hem.

Arabella could take no pleasure from her pretty clothing. She was dead and stuck in some necromancer's workroom.

And to think that only yesterday her biggest concern had been that her generous aunt and uncle had paid far too much for the ball gown she was to wear at Friday's assembly!

Arabella stared out at the rest of the chamber she could not access. Judging from the thick, leaded windows set at the top of the walls, it was partially underground. The sunlight that flowed in was surprisingly warm and golden. She suspected that some sorcery was involved; a cellar workroom should not be so well-illuminated.

The rest of the space did not match Arabella's preconceptions, either. The benches were piled with books and mathematical instruments instead of skulls, black candles, and jars of frogs' toes and newts' eyes. On the other side of the pentagram was a cleared space, with a practice dummy standing against one wall. Weapons lay in brackets affixed to the stone walls around it: swords of all sizes, a spear, a pike. The shelving underneath held padded armor.

Apparently Lord St. Ash was more into swordplay than potion making.

Arabella scowled as she thought of the young nobleman. He had known from the start, of course. It wasn't good manners or any interest in her well-being that had caused him to help her.

No, it was his *job*.

He worked in the Phantasm Bureau of the Foreign Office. Arabella was aware that one of the Bureau's duties was banishing spirits who overstayed their welcome in the mortal world.

Spirits like *her*.

He could've sent her straight to the Shadow Lands. Arabella shivered at the thought. The Shadow Lands lurked between this world and the afterlife, a place spoken of in whispers, where lost souls and demons and who knew what else wandered.

The pentagram was preferable. Perhaps her captor had a heart after all. A small one.

Arabella tried to recall all she had ever heard of Viscount St. Ash. Surprisingly for a peer's son, it wasn't much. The other young ladies never brought up his name when discussing prospective husbands. Aunt Cecilia had glossed over him when doing the same. Her cousin Harry had dropped more detail in passing conversation, but Arabella hadn't paid much attention. She had never expected to have much to do with an earl's heir, besides the occasional pre-season dance when Lumen was thin of company. She belonged to less exalted circles.

Arabella wrinkled her nose as she turned over what little she knew of the Shields. They were a powerful magical family headed by the Earl of Whitecross. The Shields were traditionally ferromentalists, magical sword masters, but the man who had imprisoned her in this pentagram had gone in a different direction altogether.

She had heard it whispered that he walked the Shadow Lands and fought against its denizens.

What was it they called him?

The Shade Hunter.

And she'd had the bad luck to encounter him, of all people, this morning. Arabella thought of how delighted and grateful she'd been, and winced. Worst of all, she'd chattered away, never suspecting he was hatching schemes to trap her in a pentagram for his sinister purposes.

Gloomy thoughts such as these occupied Arabella as the hours whiled away. The light changed, shifting across the floor, until it was gone. Twilight filled the chamber, soft and heavy and grey.

Arabella tried to hold on to her outrage, but by that time she was resigned to her captivity. And heartily bored.

So it was with relief that she heard sounds from upstairs—the slam of a door, the scuff of feet. He was back!

Arabella waited, but no one appeared at the cellar door. Instead, noises continued to emanate from upstairs. Several thuds vibrated through the ceiling. Was he dropping books or boots?

Annoyance rekindled inside Arabella. By the saints, she may be a ghost, but she was still a gentlewoman! How dare the unmannerly boor keep her waiting!

Arabella leapt to her feet and shouted, "Help! I'm down here! Help!"

Since she had no throat to feel parched, Arabella thought with malicious glee that she could keep yelling all night. *If he doesn't come soon, I promise that I will* haunt *him.*

The door at the top of the stairs crashed open, then slammed shut. The cellar steps creaked as Lord St. Ash ran down them. Rune lights bloomed yellow in the glass-sided lanterns set into the wall ahead of him.

Arabella put her hands on her hips as His Lordship's stockinged feet came into view. The rest of him followed, until a tall, lean man with tousled blond hair and wary grey eyes stood before her. His cravat was loosened and the plain brown vest he wore over a white linen shirt was unbuttoned.

Incongruously, he held a sandwich in his left hand.

"You," she informed him frostily, "forgot about me."

"And you," said St. Ash, "have a very penetrating preternatural scream." He grimaced. He had, Arabella realized, a very expressive face. It was quite different from the stony demeanor he'd put on at the supper dance.

"I apologize for that," said Arabella with dignity, "but you left me no choice." She gestured at the pentagram.

St. Ash's eyes narrowed as he surveyed her. Arabella had the impression that he was making up his mind about something. She began to feel nervous. If he decided to thrust her into the Shadow Lands after all, there was nothing she could do about it.

Apparently she passed the test, for St. Ash said lightly, "You were quite safe down here, Miss Trent, if a trifle bored."

"I should like an explanation, Lord St. Ash—" began Arabella.

"Trey," he interrupted.

Arabella frowned at him.

He waved the sandwich at her. "I'm not used to all this 'Lord this' and 'Milord that.' It puts me off my food."

Arabella remembered that he was actually the younger son. Hadn't Cousin Harry mentioned his older brother had died last year?

Still, she couldn't call him by his *name*. What would Aunt Cecilia say? She ignored his improper request to ask a more pressing question. "Why did you stick me in this pentagram?" she demanded. "I'm not going to harm anyone. Not even Priscilla Price, who called me a rustic mushroom last month."

"Did she indeed?" He looked amused. "But, you know, she's only like that towards those she perceives are a threat to her matrimonial ambitions."

Miss Price was one of Lumen society's acknowledged beauties. Arabella's eyes widened. "Was that a compliment?"

"Well, you are rather pretty," he owned. "But I've been told, by Miss Price herself, that I am no judge of these things."

"I *was* pretty," said Arabella gloomily. "And now I'm this." She gestured at her aethereal form.

"Don't be so cast down. There's hope yet. As it turns out, you're not *completely* dead."

"What do you mean, sir?"

"Just that your comatose body is safely ensconced in your bedchamber right now."

Arabella's head spun. Lord St.—Trey was a blur in her vision. "What?"

"Are you going to faint? It'll be the first time I've seen an apparition fall unconscious. I should take notes." The dratted man put his sandwich on his worktable and shuffled papers.

"Of course I'm not! Please stop teasing and tell me properly." Despite herself, her words ended on a tremble.

The laughter vanished from his face. "Poor girl." His voice was gentle. "What a trying day you've had. Why don't you sit down?"

A grey mist appeared inside the pentagram and solidified into the shape of a chair. Arabella touched the back of it, expecting her fingers to go through it.

They didn't. The chair felt smooth and cool, like marble.

"What is this?"

"Aether."

Arabella snatched her hand away. "Did you summon this from—?"

"The Shadow Lands? Yes." Remarkable. He spoke the name as if it were the most commonplace thing in the world. "Do sit down, Miss Trent. The chair won't bite."

Arabella did so, gingerly. The magical chair wasn't as hard as she'd expected, giving away slightly under her. "Arabella. If I am to call you Trey, you should call me Arabella."

"Certainly." Trey sat down on a bench and lifted his sandwich. "Do you mind? It's late and I haven't had supper yet."

At her nod, he took a bite. Arabella felt a familiar empty feeling around her middle. "I'm hungry? How is that possible?"

"It hasn't been long since you separated from your body. Your mind still remembers how you're supposed to feel if you haven't eaten all day." Trey devoured the remainder of his sandwich while Arabella tried hard not to stare longingly and drool. Could a ghost salivate?

"About my body, though?" she queried.

"You're still alive, though barely. Apparently, you slipped out of the house last evening without anyone knowing, dressed in your plainest clothes and a hooded cloak, like a girl on her way to an elopement." He raised his eyebrows. "Were you eloping?"

"Of course not," said Arabella crossly.

"Your aunt will be relieved. About dusk, you were hit by a hackney, according to a servant girl who witnessed the incident. You had run into the street after a stray kitten. You really are that kind of person, aren't you?" Amusement was writ plain on his face.

"Better than being a heartless monster," she flashed back. Goodness, he made her seem like a complete ninny. And he was the rudest man she had ever met.

He didn't rise to the bait. "Do you remember anything from last night?"

Arabella tried, but there was a horrible blank stretch where her memories of yesterday evening should be. "I remember the dressmaker bringing my ball gown in the morning. We had stewed rabbit for luncheon. I visited with Charlotte and Viola and we talked of our excursion to Shrine Park. But after that…?" She screwed up her eyes, trying to force *something* to come to her.

"No need to try so hard. You'll sprain something," Trey advised her.

Arabella frowned. "If I was hit last evening, how come I was at Shrine Park this morning?" Her friends' silence this morning made sense. She'd thought it was because they weren't used to early hours. In actuality, they hadn't been able to see her at all.

Still, they had gone on an excursion that she had wanted, most likely for her sake. The thought touched her.

"Your spirit knew where it was supposed to be this morning. With or without your body, it went."

"If only I could remember what happened in the gap." Arabella pressed her hands over her eyes. The gesture felt strange, cool and jelly-like. Arabella hastily removed them.

"It's not uncommon for spirits to lose the memories surrounding their violent deaths. Or, in your case, disembodiment."

"But my body is alive. Does that mean I can return to it?" She had clasped her hands together without realizing it.

"With a little help, I don't see why not."

A rush of relief swept over Arabella. "Thank you! Shall we go right now?" She was on her feet.

Trey waved a hand in a sit-down gesture. "Not so fast, Arabella. It's not late enough—your family and servants will still be awake. We'll leave after midnight."

"Why the secrecy?" demanded Arabella. "My aunt and uncle will not eschew your help. I know they must be anxious and concerned."

"We'll keep this secret because I'm not supposed to be doing this." Trey's face lacked expression, and she saw, for the first time, the tired lines etched into it. "By the laws of the land and the rules of the Phantasm Bureau, I should've sent you on your way to the afterlife already."

"But I'm still alive!" cried Arabella, appalled.

"Only because your aunt and uncle hired a sorcerer to put your barely-breathing self into stasis. That, by the way, comes very close to flirting with necromancy. Some would say that it crosses the line." Trey paused. "Like, for instance, my supervisor."

It all felt like a bad dream. "Will they get into trouble?" Arabella whispered.

"Only if they're caught. Right now, all they've put out is that you're unconscious after a bad accident. There's precious few people who can tell your spirit's gone wandering. And as long as any of them besides me don't peek into your bedchamber, you're safe."

Arabella stiffened. "Are you saying, sir, that you *were* in my bedchamber?"

"Of course. I had to see for myself if your body was worth returning to. And your nightclothes are very fetching, as well."

She eyed him, suspecting he was laughing at her again. Yes, that crook of his mouth and those lines around his eyes all indicated mirth. "I cannot believe that my aunt allowed you into my bedchamber."

"Of course not. Charlie Blake distracted her while I went up to check."

"*Charlie* Blake? Do you mean Charlotte?"

"She's going by her Christian name now, eh?" He shook his head. "Well, I've known her as Charlie for years. Her older brother was up at Holyrood with me and I spent some of my holidays at the Blakes."

Holyrood University was where people with magical gifts were educated. "I have met Mr. Blake on occasion," Arabella owned. "He's a pyromentalist, isn't he? I've never seen his salamander, though."

"He works two stories below me now," said Trey.

"Did you tell Charlotte about this?" Arabella made an eloquent gesture toward herself.

Trey shook his head. "No. The fewer people who know, the better. All I told Charlie was that I sensed something wrong and tracked it to your house. She didn't ask any questions, just demanded I do my utmost to help."

Arabella gave a laugh that was almost a sob. "That's Charlotte all over."

A frown deepened between Trey's brows as he looked at her. "Jonathan Blake's a reliable chap, and I gave him the details about you. If anything happens and I'm not there, go to the Blakes' house. He won't be able to see you, but his salamander will. Ember's clever; she'll help you out."

"What awful things do you expect will happen?" said Arabella. The sinking feeling was back.

"None at all," said Trey promptly. "It's just a precaution. Chin up, Arabella. By tomorrow morning you'll be waking up with a bad headache. You'll be back to extorting money for Lady Holmstead's orphans in no time."

His matter-of-fact tone was surprisingly bracing. Arabella lifted her chin. "I won't forget those hundred pounds, my lord."

Trey cracked a smile. "Good girl." He stood up, stretched his arms above his head, and yawned. "Now, if you'll excuse me, I'm in need of a few hours of rest."

"What about me?" squeaked Arabella.

"This house is well-warded. No phantasmists will be able to sniff you out nor any necromancers summon you." She knew he was pretending to misunderstand. "Just stay here." He added kindly, "I'll leave the lights on for you."

And before Arabella could object to remaining confined in the pentagram, he was gone.

At least he'd left her the chair.

Chapter Three

AT A QUARTER TO ONE in the morning, Trey stamped his feet into his boots and summoned Miss Trent.

There was the merest flicker in the air, and Arabella appeared in his front hallway. By the light of a rune-embedded magical lantern, she glimmered a faint green and floated three inches from the floor boards.

She looked first astonished, then reproachful. "You could've come down to fetch me."

Trey shrugged into his top coat. "This was faster."

Arabella looked around with interest at the wooden paneling and floral wall paper. Trey wondered why she bothered; the hallway was narrow and low-ceilinged, and both paneling and wall paper showed signs of wear. It was good enough for a bachelor's lodgings, but dingy compared to what she was used to.

"Don't you have a valet?" asked Arabella, her gaze returning to him. She came gently back to the ground.

It wasn't fashionable for gentlemen to own clothing they could get into without help. Trey, on the other hand, rated practicality higher than fashion. His relatives didn't agree; thanks to a well-meaning but meddling cousin he did actually own coats that clung to his shoulders and boots that made assistance necessary. "I have a Nat," he said. "My manservant. He's away for his grandmother's funeral in Grenwoodshire right now." He paused, counting. "Man's an oddity. This is the fifth grandmother he's buried in five years."

Arabella gurgled. "What an interesting character! I should like to meet him."

"Well, you won't get to," said Trey dampeningly. He tugged on worn leather gloves and surveyed the debutante, who looked just as charming and ghostly as she had this morning. His brows drew together.

Darn those dimples. And was it really fair for a spirit to have such long, curling eyelashes?

"Pay attention," he said tersely. "Before, it was daytime and you were protected by your obliviousness. It's altogether different at night and you've been out of your body for longer. So—Arabella, are you listening?"

His guest had plunged one incorporeal arm through his wall. She looked dispassionately at the limb, then withdrew it. Her lips pursed. "Tastes like pepper," she muttered. She stuck a toe into the oak paneling on the bottom half. "Mmm, more like home-brewed ale."

"Don't get used to it. You'll be back in your body soon enough." He wound a woolen scarf around his neck and jammed a sadly misshapen beaver hat on his head.

Several of his relations would've disowned him on the spot, had they been present.

"I'm sorry." Arabella put her finger to her lips. "You were saying?"

"Just stay close." Trey opened his front door to chilly darkness, lit only by widely-spaced gas lamps.

He felt the nearness of the Shadow Lands as soon as he stepped off his front stairs and onto the pavement, away from the safety of his wards. They hissed unhappily as he and Arabella left. The other realm had moved in and it was hungry.

The boundary between worlds was thin tonight.

Arabella seemed to feel something of the same for she moved in closer, pressing up to his arm.

White sparks flashed between them. Arabella jumped like a scalded cat, landing atop the iron railing that stretched in front of the row houses. She looked down at him in amazement.

"Stop playing," said Trey, "and come down."

She hopped off and drifted gently down to the ground. "What happened?"

"You got too close to my personal wards. They were keeping you from possessing me."

Arabella lifted her chin. "I have no desire whatsoever to possess an unfashionable, rude person such as yourself, sir."

"You forgot disagreeable. You really have no craving to suck my blood? Or tear off my face?"

She shuddered. "Not in the least."

"Good." He had seen her run through a gamut of emotions from fear to exasperation to anger, but not a single one of them had corrupted her, in spite of his testing provocations. "But if you should change your mind—"

"I won't," she said firmly.

They walked in silence down the street of darkened two-story townhouses, older, darker, and smaller than the gentry's Lumen homes. Most of Trey's neighbors were middle class: lawyers, bankers, merchants, and other government employees like himself. The neighborhood itself was unfashionable, but it was quiet and near the Quadrangle. Trey had no desire to keep a town coach for the long trip from Shield House to the city proper every day, and he could live with his relatives' disapproval over his choice of lodgings.

He considered it an advantage that they were less likely to visit him here.

Arabella glided close to him, looking around with wide, dark eyes. She seemed to be straining for something.

"Don't," said Trey quietly. Arabella started. "Don't look for signs of the other realm. Sometimes, just bending your thoughts on it brings it closer."

She nodded. Her clothes had changed again, he noted. She now wore a dark cloak and a nondescript gown beneath it. No gloves, interestingly. She'd not worn any with the shrine cloak, either.

Trey's breath misted in front of his face. He thrust his hands into his pockets, his fingers crooked to shape aether to his will. A heavy presence hung over them, breathing down his neck. The pools of yellow lamplight were faint and far away.

His own muffled footsteps and soft breaths were the only sounds in the world. Arabella was a pale glimmer next to him. Consciously or not, she had dimmed, making herself smaller and harder to see.

As she should. An innocent spirit like her was defenseless against the greater haunts who clung to this world and the demons who prowled the boundaries, hungering to get in.

The thin wail of a small child was like a vapor in the vast night, swallowed into silence. A small light skittered across their path and tumbled into the road with a whimper. It gleamed once, then vanished on the far side.

"A wisp," breathed Trey. "Not a spirit, but created when strong emotions touch the boundaries. Most dissipate within a day or two."

Arabella nodded.

A wisp wouldn't be much trouble, but just in case he'd send Morgan and his new apprentice after it tomorrow. It'd be good practice for the boy.

What worried him more was that palpable sense of being watched. The back of Trey's neck prickled. He wanted to track it, chase it down, face it head on, but… He glanced at Arabella's huge eyes. He had to get her safely back into her body first.

Despite his verbal assurances, time was running out for her.

They turned a corner and the pressure lifted with a sudden pop. Arabella gasped. Sound rushed in to fill their ears—the clatter of hoofs and wheels on cobbles, the yowl of an alley cat, the snatch of a song as drunkards staggered home from an evening of dissipation. Even the gas lamps burned all the brighter, sylphs fluttering like moths around them.

Something stirred near a heap of stone, slow and dark. A low grumble tickled the edge of Trey's hearing. A stana, an earth elemental, that had probably been hauled in from the countryside along with the building materials.

This was normal night time in Lumen.

Arabella relaxed, drifting further away from him. "This isn't so bad," she remarked.

"No." The Shadow Lands had retreated, but Trey remained watchful. *Something* had marked their presence. Something intelligent and malicious and quite likely powerful.

Something he'd have to fight and defeat.

Soon, he promised it. *I'll be your opponent soon.*

Their progress to Bottleham was swifter now. Arabella had lost her sickly pallor; she chattered all the way to her home. Trey listened with one ear, making noncommittal noises at the appropriate times. He suspected she was trying to relieve her own anxiety.

When they turned onto Crescent Circle, Arabella tilted her head toward the mews in the back. "There's a chestnut tree behind the house, right in front of my chamber window. You could climb that."

"What a scamp you are," Trey remarked. "Is that how you snuck out of the house last evening?"

"Maybe." She dimpled. "Can you climb a tree, though? You can't get much practice, living in Lumen."

"I believe I can manage. However, I'm not in the habit of entering the bedchambers of young ladies through the window. We'll take the back door."

Arabella followed him through a narrow alley to the back of the row. Trey counted houses until he came to the servants' entrance of the Elliots' residence. She peered over his shoulder as he sketched a rune in the air. It winked silver and flowed into the lock.

Trey pressed down on the handle, and the door opened with a click.

"That's it?" asked Arabella from behind him.

"That's it."

"It doesn't seem at all fair that you can do that," she said softly. She had no breath, of course, but her presence was a cool tingle on his skin.

Trey soft-stepped into the narrow corridor. "Then it's a good thing I'm on your side."

An odd sensation had settled over Arabella as she glided through the house, leading Trey up to her bedchamber via the servants' stairs. The house was at once familiar and strange, as if slumbering under an enchantment. She moved through it like she was in a dream, making no noise on the steps, stirring no air with her passage.

The steps. Remembering, Arabella stopped at the third stair from the top. She turned to Trey, pointing down at it. Then she raised a finger to her lips.

That step creaked.

Why was she bothering to keep quiet? It wasn't as if anyone else but Trey could see or hear her, anyway.

The thought was quite lowering.

Arabella flitted through the quiet second story, past the balustrade that overlooked the foyer below. The paintings of Uncle Henry's ancestors were swathes of darker shadow against walls bleached grey in the moonlight filtering from above.

A loud snore shattered the silence. Arabella froze. She found she was holding her breath.

Uncle Henry.

Trey flashed her a grin and gestured. *Go on.*

Arabella knew that her uncle slept soundly while her aunt regularly dosed herself with a sleeping draught. But Harry... she cast a doubtful glance at her cousin's door. No light shone from under it, and she couldn't quite make herself go through the wall to check if he slept.

The sooner we get this over with, the better.

Arabella hurried to her own chamber, around a corner and tucked to the side of the house, looking out into the branches of a chestnut tree. Aunt Cecilia had shown it to her with an apologetic air, but she had never minded being a little removed from the rest of the family.

She stood at the door as Trey came up. He put his hand on the handle and looked a question at her. *Are you ready?*

Arabella nodded. "Let's do this."

Let's get my life back.

He opened the door and entered. Arabella slipped in behind him and the door closed again.

The first thing Trey did was to check the window, making sure the curtains were drawn shut. Then he muttered under his breath. Three golden lights floated from his hands to three points around the simple four-poster bed.

Her bed.

Arabella forced herself to look down at her own prone body lying there, so small and stiff under the coverlet.

It was like looking at a stranger—a very young stranger. Her face was pale, her lips bloodless. A dark bruise spread from her left temple and down her cheek. The implied violence of it made Arabella shiver.

In contrast, her dark hair was neatly braided under a pretty lace cap she recognized as one belonging to Aunt Cecilia. A starched white night gown was buttoned up to her neck and the coverlet drawn up chastely to her shoulders.

The whole effect was ghastly, as if she were a corpse laid out for her funeral. Arabella wanted to move away, but her legs had turned to jelly.

Trey bent over the girl on the bed, muttering half under his breath. His grey eyes were narrowed and focused, studying things Arabella couldn't see.

She squinted and looked closer. Almost, she fancied, she could make out a dark blue glimmer all over her body.

Was that the stasis spell?

"Aha," Trey said on a soft exhalation. He held up his left hand, index finger and thumb pinched together. "Found a life line. You are not completely disembodied, Miss Trent."

Arabella couldn't see that he held anything at all. "If you say so. Did you doubt you'd find one?"

"There's always the possibility," said Trey. He moved his hands, as if winding invisible thread.

"What would you have done then?" she persisted.

He leveled his grey gaze at her. "Not much left to do if that happens."

Arabella crossed her arms and hugged herself. Her substance was chilly, but she couldn't help fidgeting, as if to make up for the unnatural stillness of her body.

Her gaze ran over the rest of the chamber, a pretty room for a young girl, with its pale golden floor, apple-green and milk-white striped wallpaper, and simple furniture. She had thought it the loveliest room when she'd first come to live with the Elliots, and still did, despite her growing experience of finer apartments. For it had been set aside, scrubbed and cleaned, and made over with love—just for *her*.

An ache constricted Arabella's throat. Her elegant orange and cream ball gown was draped on a chair pushed to one corner. The clothes press stood next to it in solemn dignity. Silver-backed brushes and glass jars lay scattered in merry confusion on her delicate marble-topped dressing table. Across the room, near the window, was her writing desk, a half-written letter to her cousin Beatrice peeking out from underneath the latest volume of a romance Aunt Cecilia had said she *must* read. The prayer niche, a narrow recess in the wall by her bed, was full of slips of paper.

Prayer notes, only some of which were hers. Her eyes stung to see them. Her family and friends had placed them there, begging the God-Father for her healing.

Could a ghost cry? Arabella would rather not find out with the Shade Hunter, cold and frowning, standing nearby.

Runes flared as Trey worked in silence. Arabella found herself listening to the small sounds of a house settling at night in the city—the tiny creaks, the sharp cracks, the rustle of little creatures and the muffled noises from outside.

Somewhere in the distance a bell rang. Was it three o' clock already? But no, the bell tolled on past the count, each distant ring hanging in the air with an otherworldly clarity.

Arabella started.

The sounds came from the Shadow Lands.

Her fingers shaped a sign of protection. *Saint Margrethe*, she begged, *help me.*

Trey looked up sharply, brows drawn together. Arabella instantly dropped her hand.

If he suspected, if he'd seen, he didn't say so.

He beckoned. "Come."

Arabella glided around the bed and stood next to him, hesitant.

Trey turned to her. "This might sting, but hold still." He placed his hands just above her shoulders.

He was uncomfortably close, his wards hissing a warning at her. Arabella didn't know where to look, so she settled for a vague stare over his shoulder and tried not to squirm.

Her shoulders twitched as a tingle ran through her. Trey turned and leaned over her body again. More runes glowed in the air, then spun into three fiery points that sank into the motionless girl's head, chest, and lower abdomen.

Arabella pitched forward as three invisible lines tugged at her. With a gasp, she braced herself, difficult to do without the traction of her feet against the floor.

"Anchor points to help you settle right in," Trey explained. "Go on, then."

"That's it?" asked Arabella suspiciously. "No burning candles or eerie chants?"

"Should've called a necromancer if you wanted that," he said tersely. "Let's get it over with."

Of course, he was looking forward to being nodding acquaintances with her once again. Well, so was she.

"I'll see you with my own eyes in a moment," she said and let herself fall forward.

Arabella had expected to drift down and sink into her body, letting her spirit flow out to the tips of her fingers and the soles of her feet.

Instead, she slammed into what felt like rock.

Arabella bounced off her body and spun crazily, misting through her bed, a chest, and finally, halfway through the floor. Her mouth was full of the taste and texture of wood shavings and her skin felt sticky with pine sap. With a groan, she pulled herself out of the floor and righted herself.

"What happened?" she demanded, feeling disheveled and bruised and put upon.

Trey stared at her, mouth open.

"That was," he said, with wholly inappropriate awe, "the least graceful thing I've ever seen a ghost do."

Arabella scowled at him. "Never mind that! Why didn't it work?" She gestured crossly at the bed.

"At a guess? There's something you need to do before you can return to your body."

"Such as?" Arabella hovered a few inches above the floor, too agitated to align herself with the proper plane of existence.

"The answer is probably locked in your own memory." Trey looked as tired of this whole affair as Arabella felt.

Arabella held back an exasperated growl, along with the words, *Some help you turned out to be.* "I spent most of the evening trying to remember, but nothing came back."

Trey rumpled his hair. "There are ways to help you, but I'm afraid it's beyond my ability."

Her conscience pricked her. She knew he hadn't had much sleep and with the Procession and Viewing on Saturday, all of the Foreign Office must be busy.

He's taken his own time to help you, against the rules. Be grateful, Arabella.

She tried to be, but it was hard.

"So, what do we do now?" she asked, trying not to sound defeated.

"See if we can find any signs to indicate what went wrong." Without warning, Trey flipped the covers back from her body.

Arabella stiffened in instinctive outrage. She opened her mouth to reprimand him, then stopped. There was something wrong with the pale hands modestly crossed over her breast, making her mortal form look like something that belonged in a crypt.

"My ring," she whispered. "My ring is missing."

"Tell me about it." Trey's eyes gleamed suddenly, weariness banished from his face.

Arabella brushed the bare place on her body's right ring finger with a spectral hand. A pressure mark encircled the base of it. "It's a sapphire, in a silver setting. I always wear it. It belonged to my mother."

"Do you think your aunt removed it?"

"No, she wouldn't have. She knows how much it means to me."

"Stolen, then." Trey gave a slow nod. "It makes sense, in an upside-down kind of way. It's almost an extension of you. Without it, your body doesn't fit right."

Arabella looked down, her ghostly hair falling down like a curtain, her field of vision narrowed to those white hands and that thin face on the bed. The fingernails of her body were tinged slightly blue, and the skin stretched over her hands had taken on a fine translucent quality.

She didn't need Trey to tell her she was dying

"How long?" she whispered. "How long do I have?"

She felt him assess her, to see how she would take the news, if she would transform into the hag he half-expected. She would've laughed at the thought if she weren't so numbed already. It wasn't worth it to prolong her own life or get vengeance by attacking him.

"Two days, I'd say. Maybe three. It's hard to judge these things."

A chill wind seemed to cut through her soul, raising a mournful howl. So it was already too late.

"It's not too late." Trey echoed her thoughts. "Come, Arabella. Let's go back and see if we can prod your memory into giving us any further hints."

Shadows crept around her, muffling his voice.

"Leave me," she whispered. "Let me be with my body." All she could think of was this barely-breathing girl, so small and waxen, like a goblin death doll. She couldn't bring herself to leave her. Possessiveness took over her—the body was *hers*.

And *he* wanted to drag her away from it.

"Arabella," Trey said, voice tight, stern. "You're letting yourself be influenced by the other realm. Come with me."

Through the fall of her hair, she saw him reach for her.

She flung herself away, crossing the room in less than an eyeblink. "No! You just want to throw me back into that pentagram!"

Trey went into a crouch, his left hand reaching for an unseen weapon. The pressure changed around Arabella, and the very air felt different, greasy and tingling.

"Arabella, I don't want to—"

"Liar!" Her voice rose to a shriek. "Just leave me alone!" She saw him spring, but she was faster.

She whirled and dived for the wall. The green and white stripes, poison and bone, loomed large in front of her.

Trey's fingers snagged the edge of her substance. A shock rippled through her, like lightning sparking in water. Arabella threw herself forward, tearing out of his reach. Her mouth tasted of glue and chalk as she fell through the wall and tumbled into the night.

Trevelyan Shield was a phantasmist, a magic user who could handle both aether and the more potent phantasmia. He was also the only Border Walker in Vaeland, a phantasmist who could roam the Shadow Lands in his corporeal body.

But he had not yet figured out how to walk through walls.

Arabella Trent slipped through his fingers, her ghostly substance stinging along his palms. An instant later, he crashed shoulder-first into the wall.

"Saint Bastien on a stick!" he snarled, staring at the place she'd vanished.

What the blazes was that bird-witted girl thinking, rushing out on a night like this?

They'd eat her alive.

Trey commanded his lights to follow him and flung open the chamber door.

A dark-haired youth stood in the oblong of yellow light, fully dressed but rumpled looking, lines etched in a harrowed face. His bloodshot eyes widened in comic dismay. "L-Lord St. Ash!" he stammered.

"Out of the way," said Trey through gritted teeth. "Your fool of a cousin—" He brushed past Harry Elliot.

"Wait!" Elliot seized Trey's sleeve. "There's something I think you should see."

Trey turned. Elliot mutely held out something small and grey.

It was a lady's reticule.

"I think you'll find an answer in there," said Elliot.

Chapter Four

ARABELLA FLED THROUGH THE STREETS of Lumen as if the Wild Hunt was at her heels. She raced through Bottleham and into the confusing tangle of the old shopping district. Streets wound, dark and serpentine, in front of her. Shadows pooled in the corners. Sometimes she waded knee-deep in the thick porridge of the street, cobblestones grinding through her. At other times, she skimmed several feet above the road. Once, she threw herself through a lamp post. It left a smear of rust on her soul.

Her back felt exposed and unprotected. At any moment, she expected a shout and a jerk back into the pentagram, to be bottled up again.

No and no and no.

Never again. She wouldn't be locked up ever again.

Her panic grew the further she lost herself in among the shops. Windows gleamed like eyes at her; doorways were shadowed entrances to unnamed horrors. Wooden signs showed symbols she could only half make out—they might've been runes written in maidens' blood and knife strokes for all she knew.

The buildings leaned over her head, blotting out the open sky.

Something scuttled in the thick gloom.

Blood pounded in Arabella's ears. *How can that be?* she thought, half-hysterical. *I have no body to carry blood around in!*

She looked up at the faint wash of stars beyond the looming structures.

Of course! Why am I hugging the ground? I'm a ghost. I can fly!

No sooner had she thought this, than a great lightness came over Arabella. She rose into the air, burst out from among the roof tops, gables, and chimney pots.

Lumen spread out like a light-dotted carpet beneath her. Arabella laughed and ascended, arms wide out to embrace the whole city. The air was sharp and clear and thin, like a glass shard. The stars pinpricked it in bright points, far above the city's smoke and lights.

Arabella drifted. To her left were Rosemary Street and Bond Place and Lyndon Square, filled with the marble mansions of the peerage. On her right, All Saints' Cathedral reared its square bulk to the sky. Ahead of her was the dark, wet back of the River Teme.

Arabella flew over its heaving waters, swollen with spring thaw. Black wavelets lapped and sucked at the crumbling banks. They churned around the posts of the bridges that spanned the river. Dirty ice chunks floated on the surface.

Then Arabella was over to the other side and amidst the pleasure gardens, closed and quiet in the early spring. The wooden structures that hosted restaurants, concerts, plays, and other entertainment in the summer were boarded up. Leafless trees slumbered still, and flower beds with nary a sprout or blade lay like thick scars. The fields were bare and empty, the gas lamps dark.

In the summer, this place would be filled with curiosities and thronged with people. Aunt Cecilia had regaled Arabella at length with descriptions of the delights in store for her: supper parties, circuses, inventions, mimes, masquerades, promenades.

All the things she would never get to experience.

Arabella drifted down to a wrought-iron bench. She didn't need its cold support and the metal tang of it was heavy on her tongue, but the habits of life persisted. She sat with her hands clenched in her lap and looked out at the raw emptiness. It looked blighted, just like the promise of her own future.

It isn't fair! I just started to live!

Church hadn't prepared her for this. Her previous life, with its series of dark days stretching endlessly into misery, hadn't either.

So what was left? To go willingly into the Shadow Lands and the afterlife beyond where the God-Father, the God-Son, and the saints awaited? Or to cling to a half-life here on earth, always watching, never to share in its changes and joys and heartaches?

If Trey Shield and his ilk would even let her be.

A chill wind, keen-edged, blew off the river. A shivery moan ran through the gardens, then quieted. In the silence left behind by the wind, the waters chuckled with sinister malice. The bench went from cold to icy, the chill burning through her.

Arabella caught a flicker of movement near a wooden playhouse, the canvas that covered the stage torn and pulling away from the nails tacking it down. A small figure approached: an urchin girl dressed in tattered rags, feet bare and bloodied. She stopped near Arabella and said, in a wistful whisper, "Spare me some bread, miss? I'm so hungry."

The beseeching dark eyes, over-large in the pinched face, might have been her own from so long ago. That thin frame, shivering in the cold, could've belonged to the child she had once been.

Arabella's heart constricted and she stood up. "Oh, you poor child! It's so frigid. Come here and I'll—" She stopped, her fingers still resting on the cloak she'd been trying to take off.

Her spectral cloak. With her incorporeal hands.

For the child who could see her.

The child she'd just invited nearer.

"You're so pretty, miss." The girl drifted closer, feet skimming over the short hoary grass without bending a single blade. "So pretty. I'm so hungry."

Arabella jumped up, hands out. "Stay away! Stay away… please." Her words ended on a waver.

"Feed me," murmured the child. "… so hungry…" Her eyes grew larger, sockets stretching, pupils swallowing up the irises and whites. Her face was a flimsy paper mask, with holes torn into it.

And through the holes, Arabella could see…

… *a grey city glistening with frost… towers frozen in mid-collapse… domes melted into oozing shadow stuff… a cracked bell with no tongue swinging and tolling, still tolling…*

"Pretty lady," crooned the girl, reaching out. Her thin fingers were overlong, capped with sharp nails. "Pretty lady will feed me."

Arabella slapped the hands away. She gasped as stinging pain burned up her arms.

The girl stopped, mouth gaping open into a maw as her jaw unhinged like a snake's. "… lady?"

And then her face began to melt.

Her features softened and ran like wax, shriveling away from her eyes and mouth. Darkness, gleaming with red eyes, took their place.

"Lady?" said a chorus of voices, high and low and medium, the whole cacophony of it shredding Arabella's every nerve. "I'm hungry, lady. Feed me, miss."

The girl's form unraveled. For one moment, she stood on one foot, a half-being. For an instant, the person she had been peeped out from the remaining part of her face. "Please, miss?" she whispered.

Then she swayed, tottered, fell forward.

And disintegrated into shadow substance, inky blackness splattering everywhere.

Arabella stood rooted, unable to look away.

Dark blobs showered on to her skirt and stuck. They writhed, leach-like. "Feed me!" came that ragged chorus once more.

"No!" Arabella beat the stuff off her. Blobs stuck to her hand, wriggled, clamping teeth into her.

Arabella pulled them off and threw them away, shuddering at the way they felt, fat and slimy. Her substance burned where they had latched on.

The blobs on the ground wriggled blindly towards each other and her. Whenever they bumped against each other, they merged. Then they turned hungry mouths in her direction.

"I am not your dinner!" Arabella yelled. Something white-hot blazed inside her.

She recognized what it was.

The desire to live.

Once, she had taken her courage in her hands and fought back. Once, she had taken her life back.

She wouldn't let that go to waste. She wouldn't let her younger self down.

Arabella forced the heat into her hands. A leech jumped at her, toothed maw aiming for her face.

Arabella snatched it with both hands and squeezed. A flash, and the leech crumbled to ash that blew away in the wind.

"I won't let you take me," she promised the blobs.

They took that as a challenge. They charged.

It was like fighting off an army of fast-moving slugs. Arabella flung them off her in scorching handfuls. She stomped on their smoldering comrades, feeling them squish as they burst into pinpoints of white fire.

Fire which affected nothing in the mortal plane. Last year's dried brown grass stood unscorched, untrampled.

The last of the demonic leeches burst into a cloud of black motes. Arabella dropped her glowing hands to her sides, with a weary triumph, an odd sort of peace.

For the first time in this whole nightmarish episode, she felt as if she could do something about her problems.

As if she wasn't some helpless ghost.

"There's the Trent constitution for you," Arabella informed the world. "If we had a family motto, it would be something suitably martial, like *Never surrender.*" She giggled at the thought.

She'd find that ring, if she had to scour all of Lumen's streets for it. She'd start at the place her body had been found, poke her nose in every nearby house, look over the shoulder of every suspected thief.

Arabella turned to go.

The attack missed her by a hair's breadth.

Something sharp and curved, glistening black, streaked past her shoulder. The air bled blue where it cut through it.

Arabella squeaked and jumped away, fear lending her wings.

A huge insectoid shape, thrice her size, faced her. Trapped colors struggled in the bulging black of its eyes. Its multi-jointed body was covered in an obsidian carapace. It stood on its back four legs; its front two were curved into the wicked blades that had nearly pierced Arabella a moment ago.

It swung its head in her direction and lunged.

The creature moved *fast.*

Arabella leapt into the air, fleeing across the Teme. The phantasm launched itself after her, its shape blurring into a shadowy mass.

It can fly too? Arabella felt a strong sense of injustice.

It could, and well, too. Now it arrowed into something long and lean, with huge wings and a beak that snapped at her ankles.

And change shape. Arabella misjudged her landing and sank ankle-deep into water-logged mud at the river bank. A slimy feeling, like being covered in slug trails, wriggled all over her.

She wrenched herself loose just as her pursuer, now a tentacled blob, landed where she had just been.

Too close! Arabella flung herself forward. Her mind complained that she was tired; she countered it by pointing out that she had no body to be tired with.

Still, there was that dragging feeling of being stretched thin, of being unraveled.

Hadn't Trey said something about a life line?

Trey. He had wards around his house, hadn't he? And he lived in the City, near the Keep. Arabella flew upwards to orient herself while the monster crawled on the ground in a jellied mass.

How would she ever find his house? If she strained, she might see the runes around it, but their glow would be lost at this height.

After all, he wanted to protect his home, not light it up like a beacon.

Bat shapes swooped around her, uttering shrieks. She thought they *were* bats, until one of them bit down on her arm.

Agony flared through her. Arabella screamed and tore off the spectral vermin. To her horror, her arm had lost its shape. It sagged bonelessly, trailing glowing strings of whatever aethereal substance it was made of.

She was dizzy with pain and nausea. Arabella thought she would faint, but that relief was not to be hers. The swarm dove for her again. Her first attacker leapt into the sky.

She dodged out of the way just in time. The larger mass sailed up, scattering scolding bats. They set upon it with tiny cries.

Arabella didn't wait to see the outcome. She fell to the ground, cradling her torn arm.

Where could she run? Where could she hide?

Where was *safe*?

The cathedral caught her attention, held it.

That's it. There'd be wards around the place.

The saints and the God-Father would keep her safe.

If they let her inside first.

The shadow monster dropped out of the sky and surged for her on hundreds of tiny, thundering feet.

Arabella screamed, "Trey!"

She ran.

Trey stood in the Elliots' fashionable drawing room, trying not to tap his foot with impatience, as Harry Elliot's halting confession wound its way to its conclusion. The boy sat on his mother's elegant chaise longue with claw-footed legs, head hanging in shame.

It was not an uncommon tale. A sheltered youth, away to university on his own for the first time. The excitement of making new acquaintances and indulging in pursuits hitherto closed to him. Boxing matches, horse races, cards of all kinds, all accompanied by wine or ale. Before he knew it, Elliot had gambled away his generous allowance. Desperate, he threw all his resources into one last wager, hoping it would pay off.

It didn't.

He was too ashamed to confess his mistakes to his adoring parents, not wanting to disappoint them. He borrowed money and pawned valuables to pay his debts of honor. But the tradesmen weren't easily disposed of, and now they were threatening to go to his father.

"I told Arabella about it." Elliot raised a haggard face to Trey. "I didn't mean to... but I was so down in the dumps... and she saw it... and asked me... I swear I didn't make her pawn her mother's ring! I didn't even know she was going to, didn't even know she had, until she went missing and my mother sent the servants after her and they brought her back and her reticule fell on the floor..." He shuddered and burst out, "By the saints, I wish I hadn't said anything to her!"

Trey hefted the reticule, heavy with guineas. On his palm, next to it, lay a scarred wooden counter with the number 13 scratched on it—the sort pawnshop owners gave to people they shouldn't be doing business with.

The underage, for instance.

"She went of her own will, Elliot," said Trey crisply. "Can't be undone. We can only move forward, so show some steel. Blubbering isn't going to help Arabella—or you."

Elliot looked up, startled. Trey realized once again just how unsuited he was to dealing with the finer feelings of the very young.

It made him feel very old.

"What you should do," he said, "is lay it all out before your father. Yes, I know he might ring a peal over you or worse, be disappointed, but from what I know and what Arabella said, he isn't going to disinherit you."

Elliot's lips parted in a *But*.

"You have to learn to take your punches like a man," added Trey. "You did it to yourself, but you aren't the first stripling to do so." He gave Elliot a thin-lipped smile. "Learn from it and face forward. Here, I'll take the token." He held the money out to Elliot.

The young man rose shakily to his feet. He looked Trey right in the eyes. "I ain't taking Bella's money. 'Taint right."

His face was set in resolute lines. He'd be all right.

Trey nodded and slipped the reticule in his pocket. He tossed the token up in the air and caught it again. "This'll help us put your cousin back together. Now to find the little fool."

Indignation kindled in Elliot's face. "Bella's the sweetest, kindest little thing—" he began.

Trey started, holding his hand up for silence. Elliot cocked his head, also listening, gaze darting from dark corner to dark corner.

A familiar scream pierced through Trey's skull. He winced at the intensity and pain in it.

It was soon followed by a voice yelling his name.

Arabella.

Trey snapped to attention. He held out his left hand. "Come, Sorrow!"

The wraith sword appeared, misting out of the Shadow Lands. His hand grasped a hilt the color of starlight, the short blade gleamed a sea-grey.

Elliot said, stuttering, "I-is that what I th-think it is?" Then he looked at Trey's face and inhaled. "Bella?"

"In trouble." No time to run through Lumen, trying to get to her before the other specters did. He had to take the quick way.

Trey spun on his heel. Looking about the room, searching for the best place.

Ah, right there.

He lifted Sorrow and made three neat cuts in the air. They shimmered purple.

"Don't worry, Elliot. I'll get her back," Trey told the shaken youth, and stepped through the portal into the Shadow Lands.

Spectral bats flew above Arabella's head, their high-pitched squeaks drilling into her skull. A black ooze reached out grasping tendrils from the side of a brick building; she kicked it off and kept running.

Her bigger problem galloped behind her. She dared not look back, but she strained to hear it, afraid it was getting closer.

Arabella burst out of the surrounding buildings and into the ring of paved stone that surrounded All Saints'. The edifice bristled with pinnacles and turrets. Lancet windows and pointed arches were black against its moonlight-bleached grey. It looked not so much like a place of worship, but a fortress.

It was the most beautiful sight Arabella had ever seen.

The stone crackled underfoot, green sparks fountaining all around her. The bats chittered their alarm and fell back. She nearly wept with relief.

If only the shadowy mass would also retreat.

She glanced over her shoulder just as it flowed across the paved stone. The hiss of warning runes did nothing to deter it.

Arabella pressed her mangled arm to her chest and pushed on through the wards. Pins and needles pricked her all over, intensifying with every step.

Better than falling to that thing *back there.*

Her progress slowed to a trudge. Shivers ran through her, threatening to tear her apart. Vitality bled out of her, leaving her more exhausted than she could ever remember being.

"Fight back…" she whispered to herself. "Don't… give up."

Her knees jellied and gave way. She collapsed in a heap of flowing soul-substance. For one horrified moment, she thought she would liquefy. Grimly, she held on to her sense of self.

At that moment, her hunter gathered itself into its insectile shape, front arms curved into wicked blades, and leapt.

Arabella flinched and closed her eyes. *Dear God-Father and Risen Lord and Saint Margrethe…*

She fully expected searing pain.

It didn't come.

Arabella opened her eyes.

A warrior stood between her and the shadow creature. His armor gleamed a dark grey as he took the creature's blow with one gauntleted hand. With his left hand, he swung a sword that seemed to be made of ice fire.

It sliced cleanly through one of the creature's front legs. The phantasm raised a howl that stripped every bit of warmth and courage from Arabella. She couldn't have moved an inch.

It didn't affect the warrior at all. He wielded the sword in a series of blazing movements, cutting the creature, driving it back. The monster rippled, became something with fiery eyes, huge paws, and claws several inches long.

The sword melted in the warrior's hands, covering both fists with a starry glow.

He punched the creature, hurling it across the courtyard. It scattered into a million inky droplets.

Arabella gaped.

Then he turned and walked over to her. "Got yourself into trouble, didn't you?"

Arabella stared up at Trey. "L-lord St. Ash." She couldn't keep the awe out of her voice—the title wasn't just for show, after all.

He grimaced. "I told you to call me Trey." The armor vaporized into nothing, and the glow concentrated around his left hand, lengthened, and dimmed into the shape of a dull fog-grey sword, blurry at the edges.

He looked tired and annoyed and disheveled, not at all like the warrior from a moment ago.

He'd hidden that side of him again. Arabella pursed her lips, putting the observation aside for future contemplation.

"I thank you for your timely intervention, my lord." Arabella started to rise and winced as the movement sent a flare of pain throughout her.

Trey's gaze sharpened as he took in her sadly malformed arm, still seeping. "You all right, scamp?"

"Of course," said Arabella faintly. The agony had dulled to a kind of sawing throb. She told herself it was better.

If only she could believe it.

"Let me see it." A frown bit deep between Trey's eyebrows. He turned the sword in his grasp, stabbing downward in one fluid movement. It hung in the air, not moving, when he let go of it.

"It's *quite* all right," began Arabella, backing away.

"Enough of that foolishness, please," said Trey. He put one hand on her shoulder, the other on her wrist. To her surprise, his grip was warm and solid. Gently, he turned her arm a little this way and that. Arabella clenched her nonexistent teeth.

"Hurts?"

"Perhaps a little," she admitted.

"What did this?" He probed her not-flesh with cool fingers that almost numbed the ache.

"A bat. One annoying, shrieking bat." She couldn't keep the disgust out of her voice.

"Shrikers." Trey nodded, as if he expected that. "Nasty teeth."

"Indeed," said Arabella fervently. His frown had deepened. Her heart sank. "What is it?" she asked, not really wanting to know.

"Infection. Look." He moved her arm again—carefully—to show her the place where her substance was puckered into ridges so dark a purple they were almost black.

Arabella felt that unfair twisting of her insides again. "How bad is it?" she whispered.

"It won't kill you any time soon," he said, with no irony whatsoever. "But you need purification and you need it fast. Luckily, you don't have far to go." He gestured towards the cathedral.

Arabella glanced at the edifice. Now that she wasn't running for her life, she could make out the shimmer of runes laid in the stone traceries of the windows and the decorations on the pinnacles. Some even lurked deep in the buttresses.

"Is it safe?" she asked doubtfully.

"Not completely. But I think you have a good chance."

Arabella regarded him, trying to read more into his lack of expression. She remembered the prickling of wards when she crossed the stone yard. She tried to imagine what it would feel like intensified ten or a hundredfold.

It was not a pleasant thought.

"Better get going," said Trey. "It's coming back." His gaze was back at the edge of the courtyard, among the dark buildings.

Shadows writhed and came back together into a heaving charcoal mass.

"What *is* that thing?"

"Barghest." Trey took up his sword again, not looking, the gesture easy and practiced.

"I thought they were big black dogs!" There was nothing canine about the form the barghest took, all angled legs and sharp blades protruding from the blob.

"They're whatever shape they want to be." He threw her an impatient look. "What are you waiting for?"

"I feel bad about leaving you to face it on your own," she confessed. After all, she was the one who'd stupidly run out into the night, attracted the barghest's attention, and yelled for him to rescue her. If only she hadn't lost her head back then—

Trey threw his head back and laughed. He sounded genuinely amused. "What? You don't think I can face this barghest on my own?"

"I'm saying," said Arabella, as the barghest grew far too many spines in a ridge down its carapaced back, "that you shouldn't have to. Because this is all my fault." Her wounded arm hurt all the more. Black clots moved up to her shoulder, shredding and tearing her aethereal flesh.

He grinned at her, eyes alight with a fire she couldn't understand. He looked fierce and a little scary and oddly so very young. "I was going to have to face this barghest some time, Arabella. Might as well be now as later."

The sword blazed in his hand. Grey smoke lay thick around him, then hardened.

With a yelled, "Run, Arabella!", Trey leapt in to meet the barghest. His sword clashed with the creature's bladed arms. The two tussled, sprang apart, circled each other.

Arabella cast one look at them and then up to where a swarm of shrikers still hovered above the rooftops.

The barghest and the man closed in again, in white slashes and black blades.

He was a Shield. He was the Shade Hunter. She recalled his practice area in the cellar. She had to trust him.

Her left arm was nearly all black now, and smoking. The stench was foul and acrid. Arabella quivered as the corruption creep-crawled questing tendrils all throughout her.

She *had* to go. One last glance at the fight, and Arabella turned and ran. *God-Father protect him!*

The tingle of the wards changed into an acid rush, centered around her hurt arm. Arabella turned sideways, head down, pushing through with her shoulder.

Her clothes had changed again. She wore a linen shift, ragged and frayed at the hem. Her legs were too translucent to make out details, but she knew they'd be covered with welts made by an ash switch.

Her past was breathing down her neck again.

Arabella forced herself all the way to the bottom of the stairs. She lifted a foot to climb.

A curtain of crackling white blazed up in front of her.

Arabella staggered back from the heat of it on her face. She could smell burning; looking down she saw her arm was shriveling.

The purity of the light in front of her terrified her. No spot nor shadow could survive it.

But how much of her would be left once it finished consuming?

Risen Lord, shield me.

Arabella ran through the light.

It hurt, but not like the shriker's bite. No, this was like being hit by lightning, only it went on for far longer. The light illuminated everything inside of her, searched all. For an eternity, it felt like her mind and heart had been laid bare, every thought and every feeling exposed to a majesty she had never before experienced.

It found every dark clot and speck, touched them all with it gaze. The corruption writhed and shrieked and scorched. It didn't die easily, and Arabella felt its every struggle.

Even worse was the feeling that the corruption did belong to her, that it was made up of her own petty resentments and careless thoughts. It had gained a toehold in her because she had let it.

Take it away, she begged the light, and pitiless and judging, the light did.

Arabella emerged on the other side, gasping for air she did not need. Her feet sank through stone. The steps rippled under her like the waves of the sea. It took several moments to drag herself up them.

At the top, Arabella stretched out both arms, whole and pearly, in front of her. She turned them this way and that. No corruption marred her substance. With a sigh of relief, Arabella turned her attention to the great oaken door, dark with age and banded with iron.

Best to get it over with quickly. Arabella squared her shoulders and let herself fall through the wood.

For an instant, the compressed weight of ages pressed down on her. All the hymns ever sung in this space tugged at her hearing; the myriad tastes of every prayer—salt and sweet and bitter and sour—slid across her tongue as she entered the cathedral itself.

After all the ferocity and fire, Arabella was taken aback to find the place inside was silent and still, shrouded in night. The ceilings vaulted high above, their carvings and paintings hidden from sight. The cracked uneven floor stretched ahead of her down the nave and to the darkened altar at the very end.

Arabella didn't think it right for a ghost to approach it. She stole down to the right instead, to the Chamber of Saints.

This odd place, with its nooks and corners and angled walls, was full of dark grey statues. Arabella made her way by memory to that of her own patron saint, Margrethe, who watched over maidens and mothers alike.

She stared up at the worn grey statue on its plinth. The stone itself was magic-imbued marble; it glowed softly, limning the saint's outstretched arms, simple gown, bare feet, and kind features. Margrethe appeared to be reaching down to her, palms out in welcome. Her smile was young and merry, her glimmering eyes ageless and wise.

She seemed to promise sanctuary, comfort, hope. Arabella's eyes stung and her throat had closed up. She had given so little thought to her patron saint last autumn, picking Margrethe only because the other debutantes did. Margrethe was the acceptable patron for marriageable girls and young matrons, but looking at the depth of kindness in her stone face, Arabella thought what a disservice she had done to both herself and the saint.

With a choked cry, Arabella flung herself down at the foot of the plinth. She huddled there and prayed, only half-articulated, but with fervor.

Trey found her there not long after. She raised her head as his footsteps rang, sharp and quick, in the silent cathedral. When he entered the Chamber, accompanied by three runic lights, he looked around at the statues, right hand raised in a reverent gesture.

His left hand was empty. The sword was gone.

She didn't ask if he had won. She could tell in the set of his shoulders, the fire still alight in his eyes.

Arabella stayed on the floor, knees up to her chest and her arms tight around them, as Trey approached. He stopped and dangled a small grey bag in front of her, stitched with leaf-green embroidery.

Arabella sat up straight, eyes widening.

Trey squatted, one knee on the floor. They were almost face to face. In his other hand, he held up a wooden counter. The number 13 was scored into it.

A jolt of recognition went through Arabella. "Harry," she whispered.

"Indeed. The boy got scared when he realized where you had been and what you had done. Do you remember?"

Memories rose up like a tide: Harry's haggard face, her own anxious sympathy, the sudden blazing idea, the grim determination that followed. The itch of coarse wool against her skin, the heaviness of the cloak on her shoulders. Creeping down the stairs, careful to skip the step that creaked. Easing the back door behind her, easing into the twilight. "Yes!"

"Do you remember the pawnbroker's name or direction?" Trey queried. "Can you take me?" His posture was taut, poised for action.

Arabella eyed him, wondering if that inner fire was as consuming, as scorching, as it looked from the outside. "Of course, but…"

"But?" His brows drew together.

"Trey, it's still the middle of the night."

"So it is!" His brow cleared, but his tone was surprised. And then he gave a cracking yawn, only mostly hidden behind a polite hand.

He badly needed his rest. Arabella felt strangely protective of his wellbeing, laughable since he'd just shown he could handle himself quite fine.

"Come." She rose to her feet. "The pawnshop will still be there in the morning. Let's go home."

He copied her movement, murmuring, "Let's go *home*? Not thinking of moving in, are you?"

The solicitous feeling vanished entirely. "As if I have any desire to spend more time than necessary in your cellar."

"Oh, but it's such a nice cellar."

There could be no other reply to his inappropriate levity but dignified silence. Arabella made hers as haughty as she could.

Trey leaned away from her in exaggerated astonishment. "Brr," he said cheerfully. "It's gotten chilly in here."

Jesting in church? He was really, thought Arabella, shaking her head, quite hopeless.

Chapter Five

TREY TOOK A GULP OF scalding black coffee, and gave the overcast sky a baleful look. His eyelids felt heavy and gritty.

Morning had come too early again.

It was a good thing he planned to intimidate, because no one would believe that he was anything other than a rogue. He had woken up to Arabella's inexpertly suppressed impatience filling his entire house. He hadn't even given himself time to shave, merely thrown on clothes from the disreputable side of his wardrobe. His hair was untidy, his chin stubbled, and no one would mistake the coarse jacket and trousers for anything belonging to a gentleman.

And now he stood under an awning in an undesirable part of town, bitter coffee his only fortification against the biting wind that was winter's last assault on Lumen. The place behind him styled itself as a bakery, but Trey had eschewed the stale buns and hard cakes he suspected were days old.

"I trust you slept well?" inquired Arabella, all solicitude.

Trey made a noncommittal noise. It was too early for conversation. Not even the shock of cold water on his face during his hurried dressing had cleared his fogged brain.

The ghost at his side, of course, suffered from no such discomforts. She wore a sunny yellow dress this morning, the same color as her front door. A chip hat with blue flowers and yellow ribbons perched on her head. She beamed out at a world that could not see her to appreciate it. The chilly gusts which knifed into him disturbed neither the folds of her skirt nor her happy mood.

"I see that you are one of those people who are always cross before breakfast," said Arabella kindly. "I won't bother you until you've sorted yourself out."

She was, Trey suspected, one of those bothersome people who rose with the sun, a smile on their faces, ready to sing with the birds. Saints, he was glad he would never have to live with one.

Once he got Arabella's spirit out of his house, that was.

He grudgingly admitted that she looked better this morning, glowing a healthy color. Her mangled arm from last night was back to normal. If she looked the slightest bit more faded than yesterday morning, it was no cause for alarm just yet. She'd only been out of her body for less than two days.

It occurred to him that this was the first time he'd ever concerned himself so much with a spirit's wellbeing. More and more he was finding himself in Hilda's role.

It didn't suit him at all. They needed to find another spirit seer to plug the holes the Great Incursion had left in the Phantasm Bureau.

In secret official reports, it was only referred to as an incursion. Such a small, innocuous, and understated word for what could have so easily been a catastrophe for more than just the survivors of the Phantasm Bureau.

He took another swig of coffee. Arabella's nose wrinkled.

"Don't like coffee?" Trey inquired, eyebrows raised.

"It smells heavenly, but it tastes so horrid."

After today, he wouldn't ever again have to share living quarters with someone who didn't appreciate coffee. The thought cheered him up somewhat. As the fog inside his head cleared, Trey acknowledged that it was, perhaps, time to go on with the day.

He drained the last drops and caught the eye of a serving boy lurking inside the food shop. The child scurried out, took the mug, and hopped right back in, out of the cold. No doubt he thought the customer had a screw loose, standing out in the wind, talking to himself.

Trey checked to make sure he was still in possession of his pocket watch and money pouch. He suspected the denizens of this neighborhood made a little profit on the side from petty larceny.

This foul tangle of streets was known on paper as the Fleet, but popularly referred to as the Fleece in recognition of what its inhabitants did to the innocents who ventured in like so many sheep. Gaming hells, pawnshops, and money lenders all jostled elbows, while more nefarious activities took place in underground cellars: drugs smuggled in from the fallen Goblin Empire; elven girls bought and sold; illegal magical practices, from hexes to necromancy.

Amazing that such a place existed around the skirts of All Saints'. Trey had friends in the Home Office who would have cheerfully watched this whole district burn—and tossed a log or two on the blaze themselves.

How in the world had Arabella Trent got herself mixed up with this place? And what on earth had she given up besides a sapphire ring? She was lucky she hadn't ended up on a barge down the Teme, into the Channel, and headed for the continent.

The object of his speculation showed no sign that any such misgivings had crossed her mind. But then, this was the girl who rescued stray kittens.

"Still no movement." Arabella's gaze was fixed on the shop across the street. It was tucked under its roof, as if hiding from too close an examination. The window glass was smudged and dirty; a mess of grimy objects was on display behind it. The door was thick wood, with one window set, like a malevolent eye, in the middle.

The sign had stayed stubbornly turned to CLOSED for upwards of half an hour. What was the matter with the pawnbroker? Didn't he have customers to overcharge and underpay?

The longer Trey stayed here, the higher his chances of turning into an ice block. "I'm going to take a look."

Arabella glided beside him as he crossed the cobbled street to the shop. The place looked even worse close up. One of the items in the window turned out to be a stuffed crocodile head, sadly falling apart.

"Of all the shady places in this district," he commented, "and you had to pick the shadiest pawnshop of them all. What were you thinking?"

Arabella locked gazes with the crocodile and gave a delicate shudder. "No one else would do business with me," she said simply.

"And well they shouldn't. Anyone can see you're underage, and completely green."

"Well," Arabella addressed the crocodile, "I thought this establishment was at least a bit respectable, since I saw Lord Atwater coming out of it."

Trey couldn't stop himself from throwing an incredulous look at her. "What?"

"Lord Atwater," explained Arabella, "is a Member of Parliament and a friend of Lady Holmstead's."

"I know who he is." Lord Atwater had also been a cabinet minister. He still showed a keen interest in the Internal Affairs division, which oversaw the Phantasm Bureau, of the Foreign Office.

He was also a friend of Trey's supervisor.

61

"Atwater has plenty of blunt of his own. Why would he visit a seedy pawnshop in the Fleece? Are you sure about this, Arabella?"

"It was he," she said, with serene confidence. "You see, I talked to him about Lady Holmstead's orphanage at Viola's—that, is Lady Stanhope's—breakfast two weeks ago."

Trey couldn't keep his lips from twitching at the thought of the famously well-mannered MP being talked at by the redoubtable Miss Trent. "How much did you get out of him?"

"Two hundred pounds." Arabella looked as self-satisfied as a cat.

Trey let out a low whistle of admiration. She flashed him a bright smile, all dimples on charming display. The sight disturbed him more than he would have liked.

No flirting with impressionable debutantes. Back to business, Trey. He rapped on the door.

"Wait!" Arabella lifted her hand. Her gloves matched her cheery dress. "Shouldn't we decide what you're going to tell him? You should say that you're looking for a birthday gift for your sister! And she likes sapphires and you were thinking of jewelry—"

"No one will believe I'm scouring pawnshops for an expensive gift," said Trey solemnly. "Unless I mean to steal it."

Arabella examined him. "Your aspect is rather villainous this morning," she agreed. "You should strive to look more pleasant."

"Never. Otherwise, I might find myself expected to help any number of chits standing appealingly by the street. One is more than enough for me." Having heard no answer, Trey knocked again, louder this time.

"But what will you *say* to get him to give you back my ring?"

"Only that I have come to reclaim your property. I have the token and he should've known better than to do business with you in the first place. And if that doesn't work, I shall glare at him in my scariest way." Trey tried the door handle. To his surprise, the door opened with a half-hearted tinkle from a lonely bell.

Arabella gave a merry laugh. "I should dearly love to see it. Perhaps I can breathe down his neck till he relents. That sort of thing always unnerves people in books."

"I shouldn't encourage you to haunt people, but I'll make an exception this time." Trey peered into an interior so gloomy, it looked like the place sunlight went to die.

It was also spectacularly cluttered, rather like the drawing room of an émigré goblin family. Trey edged into the chamber, Arabella drifting in behind him. In spite of his caution, he bumped into a table with slender gilt legs. The china on it rattled alarmingly and a cloud of dust flew up. Trey sneezed.

"Bless you," said Arabella. She was already halfway across the room, examining a display cabinet entirely full of cross china cats.

Trey turned his head and found himself staring at a bedraggled stuffed owl with glass eyes. "I know how you feel," he told it. "I'm the same way in the mornings." The owl didn't respond.

Arabella leaned over a scarred wooden counter, her eyes narrowed in frowning concentration as she attempted to ring the bell. Her fingers misted through the handle.

Trey threaded his way over to her, past a pedestal bearing a goblin-made tea pot, a worn chair swathed in shawls and lace, and a friendly gathering of brass-bound sea trunks. The tea pot was a surprise—he couldn't imagine what kind of hardship would induce a goblin to give up so precious a family heirloom.

At the counter, Arabella finally managed to solidify her fingers enough to grasp the handle. Her pleased expression gave away to chagrin when she realized she couldn't actually lift the thing. Trey bit back a chuckle with difficulty.

"Allow me," he began, then checked.

There was a faint but unmistakable feel in the air. A chill both gentle and alien caressed his cheek and tingled against his lips.

It was the scent of the Shadow Lands.

"What—?" began Arabella, as protective runes shone around both her and Trey. Trey gestured for silence, Sorrow already in his left hand. He moved around the counter and jerked aside the tattered velvet curtain into a back room.

It wasn't so much a scent that assaulted him as mingled pressure and temperature. Ice and fire seemed to strike his skin. That alone told him what had happened, but the rigid corpse on the floor, pale and drained, rimmed with hoar, confirmed it.

A ghoul had been here.

Arabella was a warm, anxious presence behind him. "Is it Mr. Gibbs?"

Trey cast a quick probe around the room, detecting no phantasms nor any traps they might've left behind. Any portals into the Shadow Lands had long since closed.

There were no traces to follow.

He dropped to his knees beside the corpse, noting the wide staring eyes and fixed grimace. The man had been unlovely in life, with a greasy fringe of hair, bad teeth, and pocked face. Death had not been kinder to him. His skin was shrunken tight against his bones and his limbs were in an inelegant sprawl.

"This the man?" Trey asked Arabella, not looking at her.

"Yes." She sounded shaken, but she hadn't lost her senses over it. Good, she wasn't prone to the vapors.

Trey knew what he would find, but he checked anyway. There was no life left in the man at all. Ghouls were too thorough—and greedy. And even if his spirit had lingered, Trey knew that it would be mute and unresponsive, blank eyes focused on inward horrors it could not escape.

"What did this?" Arabella asked softly.

"A ghoul." He didn't add *one of the nastiest phantasms in the Shadow Lands*. The God-Father knew she'd already had enough horrible experiences from this adventure to give her bad dreams for a while.

Arabella slipped past him, her skirt sparking against his hand. She didn't seem to notice it, her gaze traveling the shelves and surfaces.

Trey followed the direction of her stare. "Looks like our Mr. Gibbs wasn't content with just flirting with lawlessness." He stood and scanned the jars and bottles. What he recognized was all potent, used in foul magic, and strictly forbidden in Vaeland. "Mermaid scales. Pegasus blood. The excise men will have a field day with this."

None of the contraband was from the Shadow Lands. Trey should've been relieved by this, but the sight only increased his tension.

"Bileflower," Arabella murmured to herself, paler than he had seen her yet. The jar she paused at was small and unlabeled, full of blackish-purple ooze. Darker shapes floated in it.

Trey gave her a sharp look. "Not the kind of thing I'd expect a debutante to know."

Arabella blinked at him. "Oh. Well, I come from Umbrax, after all."

"Hmm." Trey was no authority on what passed for common knowledge in that unfamiliar county. Arabella's expression bothered him more than he would've admitted at the moment. He couldn't read the look in her eyes as she examined Gibbs's contraband, but if he had to put a word to it, the only one he could think of was…

… *harrowed.*

Trey bent and rifled through the corpse's jacket pockets, coming up with a key ring. "All right, then."

Arabella looked scandalized. "What are you doing?"

"Very shortly, excise men from the Home Office will be crawling all over this place," he told her, "because I'll have to report this. If we want to get your ring without them looking over my shoulder, now's our chance." The keys chimed against each other as he examined the bank of safe boxes set into the wall.

None were numbered, but he counted across until he found the thirteenth one. A key labeled 13 fit smoothly into the lock.

The safe box, though, was empty.

Trey frowned, then went to work, opening every box. One by one, he pulled them out and rifled through a jumble of watches, rings, pendants, brooches, and the valuables of dozens of wrecked lives.

There was no sapphire ring to be found. Arabella shook her head every time he dumped the contents onto a table.

Trey turned to the shelves. Covering his hands with aether to avoid contamination, he took down jars and peered behind them. Arabella, too, ghosted her searching fingers through every nook and cranny.

Nothing.

Trey poked through every pocket in Gibbs's clothing. "He might've taken it home with him," he said.

"Do you think it likely?" asked Arabella.

"No."

It bothered him. It bothered him that not an hour after she'd left this place, Arabella had been hit by a carriage that vanished into the night. It bothered him that Gibbs had been killed by a ghoul a day later.

And now Arabella's ring was gone. Trey's hand clenched. With an important personal possession, a dark magician had a range of options at his disposal.

Like keeping a spirit from returning to her body.

"Do you remember anything odd from your visit here, Arabella? Something that seemed trivial at the time? Think, Arabella."

"You mean, like runes or strange smells or sorcerous incantations?" Arabella wrinkled her nose. "N-no, though... when I entered I had to wait a little bit, because Mr. Gibbs was back here. He was talking to someone. I heard their voices." She looked around the room, as if expecting Gibbs's unknown visitor to suddenly appear.

"What were they talking about?" Trey pressed.

"I don't know," Arabella confessed. "It was all a murmur, and the other man had such a quiet voice. And, honestly, I was trying *not* to eavesdrop."

"I wish you had worse manners," commented Trey absently. A tiresome course of action was taking shape in his mind.

"What do we do next?" she asked. "Break into Mr. Gibbs's quarters?" She was trying to rally her spirits, but only succeeded in looking more waif-like than ever.

"No, I don't think the ring is in Gibbs's possession anymore," said Trey. "Nothing to do but ask Atwater if he saw this visitor or overheard something."

Arabella brightened. "Of course! I'm sure he would be happy to help."

Trey could not enter into her enthusiasm. The chances of Atwater considering his questions anything less than impertinence were very small indeed. "There's nothing more we can do here. Time to call in the excise men." He cast a distasteful glance at Gibbs's store of banned items.

Arabella looked down at the corpse, more saddened than shocked. "He was rather an unpleasant man," she said, "but I'm sorry this happened to him."

"So am I," said Trey grimly, but for different reasons.

A ghoul had killed in Lumen. Of all the places in Vaeland, a ghoul had come *here* to the place where Trey Shield lived and worked and walked the Shadow Lands.

He was being challenged.

I have to get Arabella back into her body.

And then I'm going after the ghoul.

After stashing a compliant Arabella back in his house and changing clothes, Trey contacted the Home Office via an aether bird. He waited at Gibbs's until the excise men arrived, then extricated himself from the situation as soon as he was able. A crowd of the Fleet's inhabitants had gathered by then, some curious, others sullen. Trey confirmed that the officer in charge would pass along any intelligence from witnesses, then set off for Green's.

Of all the gentlemen's clubs in Lumen, Green's was known for having the most influential membership. It boasted among its ranks cabinet ministers, parliament members, company directors, diplomats, and aristocratic magicians.

Trey's father, the Earl of Whitecross, was a member, as had been his older brother Damien. Trey decided it was worth it to use his family connections to get in to have a private word with Lord Atwater. This early in the morning, the politician was bound to be reading the latest dispatches and newspapers at Green's.

In the end, he hadn't needed to convince anyone to let him into the hallowed halls of the club. Apparently, it was the title that counted as a member rather than the title holder. Viscount St. Ash was cordially greeted and led to a chamber laid out for breakfast.

It still felt all wrong to wear the title that had been Damien's. Trey's mood blackened, and not even the excellent kippers could banish it.

It didn't help that Lord Atwater had left the club while Trey's message to see him was still en route. Trey left the kippers, grabbed a slice of marmalade-slathered toast, and hurried to the politician's office.

Atwater's clerk left him cooling his heels for over half an hour before admitting that Trey's quarry had left for meetings that would take him all day. "Because of the arrangements for the Viewing, of course," said the supercilious little man, clearly implying that Trey ought to be busy with those instead of chasing down his employer.

He was probably right. Trey left a message for Atwater, then headed up Hopechurch Street to his own workplace.

A knife-edged wind did its best to blow Trey back down the slope as he trudged up the hill to the Quadrangle. Tomorrow morning, a procession bearing some of the most valuable magical artifacts of the kingdom would make its stately way up this very hill. Similar processions would take place in other cities and towns all over Vaeland, marking the beginning of the Vernal Rites.

Ensuring that everything ran smoothly was a huge task.

Watchmen, peacekeepers, and other government officials were already out in force, marking up the pavement with chalk, closing down narrow side streets, setting wards against disruption. One caught Trey's eye and touched his hat to him.

Trey nodded—he didn't know the man at all, but he was used to being recognized on the Hill.

The Keep, an old, stubby structure of dirty stone, capped the hill. It was hard to believe that such an unprepossessing structure had been the first stronghold of the Vaelish people in their new land.

Now, it was more of a museum, a relic of a perilous past, but it was traditional for the Guardians to attune the Mirror of Elsinore within its walls. Their sympathetic magic, with the Mirror as focus, strengthened the country's magical protections.

After last summer, this year's renewal was desperately needed. Trey's mouth tightened. And now a ghoul had slipped into Vaeland under his very nose.

Trey worked at the Quadrangle, a rectangular limestone edifice built around a central courtyard. All of the Foreign Office shared the space, though some departments sprawled more than others. The Phantasm Bureau had the smallest suite on the third story.

Wards threaded around Trey, questioning and familiar, as he sprang up the steps. They dropped away as they recognized him. A gust of wind blew Trey towards the doors. One leaf opened as he came up to it, and he grabbed the handle for balance.

"Morning, Blake," he said to the brown-haired man who exited, his pleasant face uncharacteristically serious. "And to you, too, Mistress Ember." He bowed his head at the flame-colored flicker above Blake's right shoulder.

"Trey," Blake lost his preoccupied look. His gaze sharpened. "You look fagged to death."

Trey rubbed his chin—he hadn't shaved in two days. "You don't look much better." There were dark circles under Blake's over-bright eyes. His friend nodded, a tired smile on his face.

The Vernal Rites doubled the work for everyone in the Quadrangle.

Trey let the door go—it swung heavily shut. They stood in the portico, Trey with his hands deep in his coat pockets, Blake staring down at the city. Blake's salamander was a cheery yellow glow, filling the small space with warmth.

"You know how it is," said Blake. "Every church and cemetery insists it needs purification before Holy Week. Ember is in demand." He held a slip of silver paper to the fire elemental. She crackled happily as she ate, her small flames delicately licking the treat, her tail curled around her body.

Blake had always been too modest about his own skills, Trey thought. He was a surprise magician: no one else in his family had the gift. Scions of traditionally gifted families—like himself, Trey freely admitted—didn't suffer from a lack of confidence in their own abilities.

"You'll always get more requests than you can handle, even from official channels," he said. "You have to use your own judgement and not stretch yourself too thin." Trey flicked a glance at Ember, contentedly buzzing. "Ember relies on you to make good use of her powers."

Blake looked amused. "You don't look like you've been following your own advice, Trey."

"Damn right I haven't," said Trey feelingly. "But I made it my business, so I have an obligation to see it through."

Blake lost his smile and lowered his voice. "How is Arabella—Miss Trent, that is? Is she—no, of course, not. You wouldn't bring her here."

"Arabella, is it?" Trey eyed his friend. "Sweet on her, are you?"

"She's a nice little thing. Good friend of Charlie's. Wouldn't want anything to happen to her. Charlie would be upset." Blake grinned at him. "She *particularly* wanted me to tell you to treat her friend gently. Charlie knows how you can be."

"How I can be?"

"You aren't always the most pleasant and sympathetic of people, old fellow," Blake pointed out.

"Miss Trent has bigger problems than my lack of manners towards her."

"Ah." Blake looked somber. "No luck yet."

"Not much luck, but a hint or two." Trey clapped Blake on the shoulder. "Tell Charlie not to worry. I'm taking care of her friend."

"I will." And as Trey pulled open the door, Blake called, "Heard that Winter's looking for you."

"Of course he is," Trey called back. The interior was gloomy and echoing, with marble floors muddy from people tramping back and forth. A servant desultorily pushed a dirty mop across the floor. Trey headed up the three flights of stairs to where his supervisor, August Winter, waited, no doubt ready to take his tardy underling to task.

Chapter Six

THE PHANTASM BUREAU WAS ON the topmost story, next to storage rooms stuffed with rolled-up rugs and broken chairs. Their suite was small, but too empty of people and too full of memories. Trey pushed open the door and was once again assailed by the wrongness of it all.

Desks whose owners would never return were still piled high with papers. Chairs, including Hilda's big one with the indentation of her body still pressed in it, were pushed to corners and against the walls. Half-empty boxes on the floor were for personal items that no one had time to finish packing and return to grieving families.

Trey put his hat on a rack and his top coat on a peg and glanced at the only occupant of the front room. Sutton hadn't looked up, still hunched over his dishes of ink and milk and salt and fresh water. Trey didn't know if the small, thin man ever went home any more, as if his vigilance in monitoring the boundaries of the Shadow Lands was his penance for surviving the Incursion.

Trey crossed over to Sutton, casting a shadow over a small plate of milk. Sutton moved it into the light and said, never taking his eyes from the swirls of ink in it, "Winter wants to see you in his office."

Trey glanced at the shut door across the room. "Morgan out with the new boy? What'd he have to say about Jem?"

"He said, 'He'll do.'" Sutton squirted red ink into water milky with salt crystals. He studied the swirls that meant nothing to Trey.

"Anything come up recently?" Trey asked.

Now, Sutton did look up, light turning his spectacles to silver, hiding his expression. "You mean aside from the disturbance near the cathedral last night? But you took care of that, didn't you."

From Sutton's tone, Trey suspected that he had broken a number of Winter's interminable rules by his handling of the barghest last night. He probably had an unread copy of recent regulations on his desk somewhere.

"It was only a barghest." Trey shrugged. "No, I'm looking for something else that was abroad last night."

"What?"

"A ghoul."

Sutton's pinched face paled to the color of curdled milk. He swung back to his dishes, scattering powder over them, lips moving in soundless incantations.

Trey watched for a moment, then turned towards Winter's office. Might as well get the unpleasant interview over with. He had a request of his own to make, too.

He had his hand up to knock when Sutton said behind him, "You know."

"Eh?" Trey turned around to look at the man's narrow wool-clad back.

"You know, you could've called for help." Sutton's tones were neutral. "The Phantasm Bureau isn't just you."

Trey's mouth twisted as he looked around the room. "Believe me, Sutton, I remember it every time I come in here."

And he rapped on Winter's door.

August Winter had taken over the shattered and reduced Phantasm Bureau at the close of the Incursion last year. His predecessor, Horatio Halford, had been invalided out from the position. Trey suspected, though, that Halford's health had only been the official excuse. Scared politicians tended to look for someone to blame.

Trey had nearly come to blows with some asinine aristocrat for suggesting that the common Halford had been ill-equipped to deal with the invasion the way a born noble would've been. Only Blake's timely intervention had kept him from a duel that would've ended his career, Shade Hunter or no.

August Winter prized self-discipline above all.

He was a tall, lean man with smooth black hair and cold blue eyes, always impeccably dressed. Right now, he stood inside a magic circle in the corner of his office, consulting with colleagues from other branches and departments. Privacy runes shimmered in the air, blocking out all speech.

Trey had been waved to a chair to wait, but instead he propped his shoulder against the wall and looked out of the window at the dreary sky and grimy city beyond. From the corner of his eye, he grudgingly admired Winter's spellwork—the man was one of the best rune masters in Vaeland. His style was both efficient and elegant.

In contrast, Halford was entirely self-taught, his runes written in a slipshod manner, including some that he had made up. Even Trey, an independent thinker, had been startled upon first seeing them.

But it was their unique ways of looking at the world of magic that made Halford and Trey sympathetic to each other's style. If it weren't for Halford's guidance, Trey would never have found himself in government employ. He'd been far too arrogant at the time.

He probably still was.

Prior to Winter's appointment as supervisor of the Phantasm Bureau, his only interaction with Trey had been the one senior seminar the latter had taken with him at Holyrood. Both had come out of the experience with less than charitable feelings towards each other.

Now they treated each other with guarded respect and that was that. Trey was under no illusions that Winter only suffered his presence.

And he knew just what Winter would say—and do—if he found out about Arabella.

Winter finished his conference and dismissed runes with one precise gesture of his hand. He stepped from the circle and nodded at Trey. "Good afternoon, Mr. Shield." Everyone was a *Mister* in the Phantasm Bureau, regardless of birth.

Did he emphasize *afternoon* with ironic inflection? Trey's mouth hardened but he responded with chill civility. "You wanted to see me, sir?"

Winter sat in his chair and steepled his fingers. "Last night, there was a significant disturbance near All Saints'. Sutton picked up your presence in the vicinity. What happened?"

"A barghest and some shrikers," said Trey briefly. "I took care of them."

"So near the cathedral? What would cause a barghest to venture so close to those wards?"

Trey twitched a shoulder. "It is that time of the year, sir." Most people looked forward to the Vernal Rites with a sense of relief, believing that the darkness and cold of winter strengthened the demons of the Shadow Lands. Those with the gift knew that the new life of spring could be dangerously twisted by those same demons, strengthening them for a last push against the weakened defenses of Vaeland.

Thresholds, whether in between times or places, were dangerous.

Winter examined Trey in expressionless silence. Trey met his gaze with a bland one of his own. He kept his breathing deep and even, and his shoulders relaxed.

Dealing with Winter had taught Trey more composure than he would've thought possible a year ago. Their meetings tended to be terse and business-like, neither caring much for the other's company.

Pity that the Viewing necessitated daily interactions. Winter was too conscientious to forego them.

Winter looked down at his desk. Trey recognized his own message, rimmed in frost and fuzzy at the edges, upon its rich rosewood surface. All the furnishings Winter had brought in were simple, but expensive.

It didn't feel like Halford's office at all now.

"What of the pawnbroker engaged in contraband smuggling whom you discovered this morning?" Winter placed an index finger on the note Trey had dashed off to the Office alerting them to Gibbs and his operation.

Uneasy, Trey wondered how much intelligence Winter could glean from his missive. He knew only a small extent of his supervisor's gift. Winter, on the other hand, had access to all of Halford's documents on him. Trey was grateful for the latter's abrupt recording style and messy scrawl.

"He was killed by a ghoul last night." Let Winter think he'd found Gibbs while following the ghoul. "It's possible the murder and the smuggling are related. Perhaps he tried a spell that caught the ghoul's attention. Internal could help us ascertain what he might've been doing."

A frown bit deep between Winter's brows. He gave a curt shake of the head. "Internal is just as busy as we are. We'll have to take a defensive stance until the Rites are over. I'll ask Sutton to keep watch for ghoulish activity, but we cannot commit to a full hunt right now." He tapped the aether square, which curled in on itself and dissolved into motes.

Trey couldn't let Winter move on just yet. "Lord Atwater was seen leaving Gibbs's establishment two nights ago. I have yet to obtain an interview with him, though. If you could put in a word, I'd like to see him this afternoon." He hated to ask the favor but it had to be done. Arabella was running out of time.

Winter's eyebrows arched. "Lord Atwater?" he asked, incredulous. "Are you sure of this intelligence? How many of the disreputable inhabitants of the Fleet are even able to identify his lordship?"

"I have good reason to believe the witness is respectable and the intelligence worth investigating," said Trey. "A few minutes of Lord Atwater's time should suffice to tell me if that's the case."

"Very well. I shall see Atwater at a meeting this afternoon and ask him myself." Winter dipped a pen in ink and wrote out a note to himself on a sheet of linen paper. He appraised Trey out of eyes that gave nothing away. "Will that satisfy you, Mr. Shield?"

It didn't, but Trey jerked his head downward into a nod. He didn't want Winter looking too closely into the identity of his witness.

And his supervisor didn't explicitly say that Trey couldn't question the politician himself. *Though saints know that he won't be very happy to find out I went behind his back.*

"If that's all, sir…" Trey turned towards the door.

"One moment, please." Winter raised a finger. "It's come to my attention that the niece of a genteel family is being kept in stasis after an accident that occurred Wednesday evening."

Blood rushed to Trey's head, pounding in his temple. He managed a creditable degree of disinterest as he faced Winter again. "Indeed?"

"Are you acquainted with the Elliots?" What did Winter know? Saints, the man could be nigh on unreadable.

"Only a little."

"Elliot is a sensible man, but his wife is prone to a great deal of sentimentality. Unfortunately, in the matter of her niece he has been swayed by Mrs. Elliot's importunities. The niece is a Miss Trent."

Trey frowned slightly, as if remembering. "I stood up with her once. She's the girl who proses on about Lady Holmstead's orphanage."

"Precisely," Winter said with a hint of a sigh. Trey suppressed a quiver of mirth. How many pounds had that chit wrung from his cold-hearted supervisor?

One day, he'd have to track down the hapless donors she had left in her wake.

"I'm sorry to hear of her accident, but it is acceptable for victims to be kept in stasis for a few days in the hopes that they will come to."

"Three nights." Winter held up three fingers. "I can give her three nights to return to her body. If she hasn't woken up by tomorrow morning, you and Father Patrick will perform an exorcism."

Trey didn't even attempt to disguise his shock. "What? But that's the morning of the Viewing!"

"Exactly. It must be done before the Rites are completed."

"You won't let me hunt a ghoul, but you're worried about the spirit of some spoiled debutante disrupting the Rites?" He felt guilty maligning Arabella, but he had to make her sound as unthreatening as possible.

Winter leaned back in his chair, ice-blue eyes boring into his. "If her spirit still lingers, she is half of this world and half of the next. That makes her more dangerous than a ghoul right now. Remember always the Shadow Lands stand ready to exploit any opening."

"Dozens of people die in Lumen every day," Trey pointed out. "Are we going to exorcise every single one?"

"Most spirits move on without any help from us. By putting the unfortunate girl's body in stasis, the Elliots have made it difficult for her to let go. We must remove her attachment to this world."

Trey's eyes narrowed. "You're trying to make an example out of her."

Winter matched him stare for stare. "After last year, you of all people should know how dangerous it is for us to hold onto people long after we should've let them go."

Trey's fists clenched. "This is not about Damien."

"No, it's about the indulgence that leads to such situations." Winter regarded him somberly. "Miss Trent was young, pleasant, and pretty. It's natural to want to give her as much of a chance as we can. But that kind of thinking—and the latitude allowed to peers and genteel alike—led us to make several costly mistakes during the Incursion. It is *my* job to ensure there won't be a repeat of that. I will take full responsibility and the vilification that comes with it."

Trey saw the faint grey of weariness under Winter's eyes, the tiredness his ramrod-straight posture held back through sheer force of will. It made him angry, because he did not want to feel sorry for the man.

He did not want to admit that there was truth in what Winter said.

"If that is all, then excuse me. I have work to attend to."

Winter nodded. "Dismissed, Mr. Shield. But with two caveats: You are not to hunt the ghoul, and if you come across Miss Trent's spirit—"

"I will return her to her body, of course," interrupted Trey. He dared Winter to naysay him.

"That would be the happiest outcome. But if it doesn't work—you know what my expectations are."

"Of course, sir." Trey gave a perfunctory bow and quit the room. He felt Winter's eyes on him the whole time.

Trey, frowning, closed Winter's door with a rather decisive click.

The atmosphere in the office had changed. For one thing, it was rather more crowded. Sutton leaned back in his chair, a rare smile on his face. Morgan, stocky and dark-whiskered and middle-aged, stood guffawing at some joke. A cleaned-up Jem in faded but warm clothes fidgeted uncertainly nearby.

The fourth occupant was enthroned in Hilda's chair, left leg propped up on a footstool. A simple walking stick leaned against the chair.

Trey scowled and strode up to the group. He glared at the man in the chair. "Old man, what are you doing here?"

"Blunt as ever, ain't you boy?" Horatio Halford grinned up at him.

Trey glanced at Halford's leg. "You shouldn't be here." Halford had been lucky not to lose the limb altogether. His wounds had remained half-healed for months, causing much anxiety about amputation. Even now, the signs of ill health showed in his shrunken frame and hollowed cheeks. Halford had been a solid man with a healthy appetite for good food. Now his clothes were too large for him.

"I'm retired, not dead," Halford retorted. At least his voice had recovered, booming out the way it used to. For a month after the Incursion, he hadn't been able to speak above a whisper.

Trey gave an exaggerated wince. "So I can hear." But he was smiling now. Halford's overloud cheer had that effect on one's spirits.

"Besides, I know you can use the help around this time," went on Halford gruffly. His gaze flicked around the room, at the places his people had once occupied.

"And it's good to have you back, sir," said Morgan fervently. Morgan was a darn good agent, with a nose for those pernicious sprites and wraiths Sutton's scrying couldn't pick up.

Halford waggled a finger at his former underling. "Don't get too used to it, Morgan. I'll be returning to my roses soon enough. They don't talk back, unlike you lot." His brown eyes were full of good humor.

Morgan chuckled. Halford beckoned Jem. "Who do you have here? An apprentice?"

"Aye, sir. Mr. Shield was so good as to find him for me." Morgan put a hand on Jem's back and pushed the child forward. "This'un's a seer."

"A seer, eh? We can always use them." Halford and Jem scrutinized each other, Halford with frank examination, the latter with wary suspicion.

"Yes, he spotted a ghost I came across," Trey interjected, with a warning glance at Jem. The boy noted it and held his tongue about Arabella.

So did Halford. He didn't say anything, but the way he quirked his eyebrow showed that he wouldn't forget to ask Trey.

"Does Winter know you're here?" Trey asked, half-turning towards the supervisor's shut door. During Halford's reign, that door was hardly ever closed.

"Wouldn't have come if he hadn't agreed to it," said Halford. "It's his turf now, boy." His gaze held Trey's. *The sooner you come to terms with it, the better*, it seemed to say.

Trey's lips thinned. He gave a clipped nod. *Right. But it doesn't mean I have to like it.*

"Look like you've been through a wine press. All of you do." Halford looked around. "When did you have luncheon?"

"Half an hour ago," said Morgan. Sutton lifted up the newspaper wrappings of his own lunch.

"I got breakfast," muttered Trey. "And coffee."

Halford grasped his walking stick and heaved himself up to his feet. Trey noted the slight tremor in his hand, the momentary blanching of his weather-beaten complexion as Halford put pressure on his injured leg. "Then you can accompany me to the Lion for a bite." It was a command, albeit not one that Trey would've resisted.

Some time alone, and he could ask Halford for advice about his ghost problem.

Chapter Seven

Arabella drifted through the first story of Trey's house with far more interest than was seemly.

She resigned herself to the idea that she was, after all, a rather inquisitive young woman.

When else in her life would she have the opportunity to examine a bachelor's living arrangements so thoroughly?

Trey had refrained from putting her into the pentagram after extracting a promise of good behavior. She had solemnly vowed to stay inside and not test or play with his wards. In his hurry, he had forgotten to give her any rules for her behavior *inside* his abode. Arabella had not reminded him.

She'd started with the cellar workshop, her ghostly hands behind her back as she studied the array of weapons, piles of books, and rows of instruments she had no name for. She knew better than to touch, even with insubstantial limbs, any of a magician's accoutrements.

Once she'd satisfied herself that he was no practitioner of black magic, Arabella glided up to the dingy hallway. Out of habit, she glanced at her reflection in the spotted mirror that hung by the coat rack.

Only an empty hallway looked back at her.

A feeling of unreality nearly overcame her. She had no insides, but they still insisted on tightening anyway. Arabella looked down at her translucent form, doing her best to ignore the floorboards she could see through her lower half.

She closed her eyes and pictured herself in her favorite morning dress. When she opened them again—how had she not been able to see through her transparent lids?—she wore a spotted muslin gown with lace at the neck and cuffs. This was the first pretty dress she'd ever owned and it gave her courage like no other.

A thought struck her. Inspired, Arabella called up a mental image of Priscilla Price's golden curls. She squinted down at her own hair, its tendrils lying on her shoulders.

Still dark. Oh, well. It seemed that there were limits to what changes to her physical appearance her spirit would accept.

Arabella chose a closed door at random and dove through it. A shivery feeling of oak and smoke ran through her. She was in a silent, surprisingly clean kitchen. Rows of polished copper pots and pans hung from hooks. An iron sink gleamed. A blackened oven squatted in one corner. Arabella poked her head into the larder to her right. All she saw were a stale loaf of bread, a rind of cheese, and some old potatoes and onions.

Arabella tried to picture Trey bustling around in the kitchen and failed. This must be the missing Nat's domain. She had no idea what to expect from the Shade Hunter's manservant.

A door from the kitchen opened into a tiny dining room at the front of the house. Mindful of Trey's instructions, Arabella retreated from the room and its street-facing windows.

The only other sizeable room downstairs turned out to be a sitting room, with gloomy wallpaper and uncomfortable, prim-looking furniture haughtily avoiding each other and demanding to not be sat upon or used in anyway.

Arabella didn't expect much sitting happened in that room. The dust on the mantelpiece confirmed that neither master nor manservant cared overmuch about this chamber. No, if Trey had company, he entertained elsewhere. Arabella speculated that he used this room for meeting with people he wanted to get rid of quickly. It certainly didn't invite cozy chats.

Having begun exploring, Arabella was not to be deterred by the stairway leading up to more private areas of the house. Her toes trailing through the age-worn steps, she floated upstairs.

Three doors opened off the landing. One stood ajar, and through the gap Arabella caught a glimpse of a four-poster bed, a chair piled high with clothes, and a beige wall beyond,

Do the same rules of propriety that govern the conduct of young women apply to their spirits as well? she wondered. Even after reminding herself that Trey had unceremoniously burst into her own bedchamber *twice*, Arabella couldn't bring herself to enter his. Not all the curiosity in the world could embolden her that much.

Arabella turned away and pushed through another closed door. This turned out to be a closet, and Arabella found herself neatly trisected by shelves and piles of linen. Her throat tasted of lye, and a starched feeling spread over her. She stumbled backwards, shuddering.

That left only one chamber, the one above the sitting room. Arabella cautiously poked her head through the paneled door and was relieved to find that it was only a library. She edged the rest of the way in, and stood looking about with an air of revelation.

Yes, this was certainly a lived-in room. Dozens of books crowded shelves free of dust. The tables were covered in volumes and papers. Chairs crowded invitingly around a fireplace.

Arabella examined the spines on a nearby shelf. The worn and battered books boasted names like *The Cardinal Principles of Magic*, *The Septum Arcana*, and *Doyle's Treatise on the Nature of the Aethereal*.

All of them sounded thoroughly yawn-inducing. Arabella drifted past the shelves, her eyes picking out names at random (*The Geometry of Wards*, *Runes for the Advanced Magician*) until she came to a glass cabinet.

Arabella recoiled, not from the warning flare of wards surrounding the cabinet, but from the knife-edged chill that emanated from the single book within it.

It stood on frosted glass, padlocked shut and chained to columns of silver. Its cover was of tanned hide and its title a single word slashed in letters the color of void: DAEMON.

The very name was a scream in her mind. Arabella clapped her hands to her ears and looked away. The memory of it—along with the tang of blood, the smear of rust, and the taste of despair—echoed.

At the edge of her vision, the book shuddered.

Arabella darted a sideways glance at it, unable to face it head on, yet unable to wrench her gaze away entirely.

The padlock rattled and the chains clinked. Was it just her imagination, or did the cover itself ripple as if alive? The title seemed to crawl over its surface. The muted rustling of pages came from within.

Pages? Or something else entirely?

The book jolted. Arabella froze. The world seemed to hold its breath.

Wards burned a steady blue, that terrible word washed away in the glow. The echoes in her head died. Arabella found she could move again, and move she did, hurrying to the opposite wall, almost plastering herself across the more ordinary books there.

That book's dangerous! Why does he keep it?

No, it wasn't merely dangerous.

It was alive—and evil. Even from across the room, its malice washed over her like acid.

What did it say about Trevelyan Shield that he kept such a thing in a room he spent so much time in? That he could bear to spend even an hour in its cruel, dark company?

Arabella had no answer to this. Every time she thought she knew what kind of a man he was, something changed and she had to figure him out again. The remote, haughty nobleman was also the informal young man who made jokes and lounged about in a loosened cravat. The warrior who had saved her last night was also the keeper of an evil whose emanations made her ill.

Images flashed through her mind, of a wry smile, relaxed posture, grey eyes cool or warm or laughing or gleaming with an excitement she could not share… Arabella shook them all away.

It's only natural for a young girl to feel attachment towards her rescuer. But for Saints' sake, don't lose your head over him, Arabella!

No, she planned an ordinary life for herself. She'd enjoy a couple of Seasons before making a suitable match and settling down to the normal duties of a wife and mother.

Books like the one across the library had no place in that future, and neither did their owners.

So fierce was her determination that Arabella at first misread the warmth as rising from her rush of emotions. It took her a moment to realize that it emanated from an alcove in the wall next to her.

The feeling spread like honey, something between a laugh and a tickle. It covered her in a strong gladness. Arabella peered into the niche, wondering which saint a man like Trey claimed as patron, what form his devotions took.

The niche was sparse, containing only a leather-bound book of Scriptures, a medallion with a religious symbol, and a gold locket.

Arabella examined the symbol, a long-handled knife crossed with a hook. It belonged to no saint she was familiar with, though that didn't mean much. Dismissing the medallion, she leaned over the locket with greater interest.

The locket was a pretty one, oval with pearl-set flowers and a delicate chain. It was decidedly feminine, and of the type that held a miniature and possibly a lock of hair. Arabella drew back, flushed with embarrassment. Trey was not the sentimental sort, but that keepsake must mean a great deal to him. It was all wrong to have intruded upon his privacy like this.

Arabella left the room by simply sinking through the floor. She drifted down from the ceiling of the sitting room, her mouth dry and woody. She was sure her hair was covered in cobwebs and the accumulated dust of decades.

With a shake, Arabella whisked herself into the kitchen, which seemed the safest place to lurk in. There, she discovered a stash of lurid gothic novels behind a jar of flour, presumably hidden there by Nat, who she was evincing a lively interest in. She swiped at the books with her hand, hardening her substance enough that one tumbled onto the wooden table.

Fortunately, it was the first volume of *The Castle of Ormolo*. Arabella pawed it for some time, finally managing to get it open and oriented the right way. She leaned over the fine gilt-edged pages, blowing on them to make them turn. It wasn't the best solution, as she turned several at a time more often than not. She had to resign herself to not reading pages ten and eleven, but she was soon absorbed in the trials of the beautiful Belinda Beaufort. The heroine's troubles kept her occupied until the handle of the back door rattled.

Arabella jumped, looking around guiltily, as if to ascertain that no one had caught her reading about Belinda meeting Count Ormolo at the top of a lonely tower in nothing but a night dress. She shoved the volume back behind the jar as the door eased open.

A child's face, sharp with suspicion, peered around the edge. Wary eyes fell upon Arabella, standing by the table, and widened in recognition.

"Oh," said Arabella, startled but pleased. "You're the boy from yesterday. Jem, wasn't it?"

All of Jem appeared around the door, laden basket in arms. He carried it to the table and dropped it with a grunt.

"Did Trey—um, Lord St. Ash send you?" Arabella asked as Jem shut the door.

The boy held up his right thumb, with a flickering blue rune wrapped around it. "Aye, if that's the gent's name. Everyone else at the spook 'ouse just calls 'im Shield." Jem surveyed Arabella critically. "Ye've faded," he announced.

"I suppose I have," said Arabella calmly, examining the child with equal interest. Scrubbed and cleaned, Jem turned out to have straw-colored hair that flopped down over bright blue eyes. The bones of his face were rather fine, and a sudden awareness flashed through Arabella.

"They're treating you well at the Phantasm Bureau?" she queried. The child wore a too-big rough coat, but it was clean and warm. She noted with approval his shoes and the red mittens peeking out from the coat pockets.

Jem shrugged a shoulder. "Me belly's full and me body's warm. Can't ask for more."

"You don't have to stay there forever," said Arabella. "Have you thought about school?"

"Book learnin'." Jem made a face and flapped a dismissive hand.

"Is good for you," Arabella completed. "If you wanted to, I'm sure Tr—they would let you. I know a charity school you could go to."

"Don't need yer 'elp, miss," said Jem gruffly, unpacking the basket and laying out meat pies, apples, butter, and eggs.

"Not at the moment," Arabella agreed. "But you can't stay in that disguise forever, you know."

Jem shot Arabella a hard glare. Arabella matched it with a direct one of her own.

Jem heaved a sigh. "What gave it away?" she said, resigned. "Was it wimmin's wit? Me ma could see right through a body, she could."

Arabella hid a smile. "I think it was because you reminded me of myself."

Jem looked disbelieving. "I s'ppose ye'll tell the coves at the spook 'ouse, eh?"

Arabella shook her head. "No. I hope you will yourself someday. I won't pry into why you're dressed up as a boy, but I want you to know I'm ready to help you—if you should need it someday."

"Like when I get a bosom and such," said the forthright Jem.

"Among other things."

"Huh. Ye really mean it." Arabella tried to radiate sympathy as Jem eyed her. "I thought ye were just a mawkish sort."

"I've been cold and hungry and scared before," said Arabella, low-voiced. *We're more alike than you know.*

"Well, I'll think 'bout it," said Jem magnanimously. "Though why ye're worrit about me is beyond me ken. Seems like ye got yer own troubles."

Arabella's spirits sank a little at this brutal assessment. "Lord St. Ash has the situation well in hand," she said, as much to reassure herself as Jem.

"No, he ain't," continued the relentless realist. "I 'eard him tell the cove who used to be head o' the spook 'ouse that the cove who's head now told him to *exorcise* you Sat'rday mornin'. Was right worrit about it, he was."

Arabella untangled this confidence. "August Winter wants to banish me to the Shadow Lands?"

"Aye," confirmed Jem. "Only he don't know Mister Shield's got you locked up here, jest that yer people have yer body. If he did—" Jem made a macabre, throat-cutting gesture.

A nervous hollow feeling gnawed at Arabella. She had till tomorrow morning? And Trey was the one who'd have to exorcise her?

He wouldn't—would he?

"Huh," said Jem again. "Yer as white as a sheet. Didn't think bogeys could get that pale. Mebbe I shouldn't have told ye that, but I figure a girl's gotta know." Her young-old eyes challenged Arabella. "Whatcha gonna do, miss?"

Going to do? Arabella could think of several grisly methods of prolonging her own existence in Vaeland. No doubt Trey's books upstairs could give her many more. A place like Lumen had to have its share of necromancers and witches alike. She could walk out right now and take matters into her own hands.

But how far was she willing to go?

And how much faith was she going to put in Trevelyan Shield?

"Going to do?" Arabella said aloud brightly. She smiled at Jem. "Do you know how to bake a cake?"

Jem had been gone for hours by the time Arabella heard the snick of a key turning in a lock, the rasp of the door, and Trey's firm step in the hallway. She sat with her elbows on the table, her chin propped up in her hands. The pose was harder than it looked—with her lack of substance, it was too easy to sink into a bench.

The fire that Jem had built in the oven had died to a few glowing embers.

Trey stood in the kitchen doorway, still in his top coat and hat, and stared at the row of cakes in front of Arabella. "You've been busy."

"I gave Jem half," said Arabella, "but you may have the rest."

Trey approached the table, stripping off his gloves. He lifted one of the golden-brown cakes. "Did Jem make these?" Wariness tinged his tone.

"We both did," said Arabella. She spread out her translucent hands in front of her. "These will interact with the corporeal world, but it's hard."

"From ghost to pokey in one day? Impressive." Trey took a bite of cake. His expression changed. "This is good!"

"Of course it is," said Arabella tartly. "I supervised, after all. It would taste even better if you kept honey in the house."

Trey brushed off the criticism. "Stocking the larder is Nat's job. Hmm, I see Jem brought those meat pies, though one is missing."

"Jem's payment for running your errands." Arabella gave a benevolent smile. "I said he could take one."

"Please, do not scruple to make yourself at ease in my home," said Trey dryly.

"Thank you, but I'd rather not." Arabella tilted her head and regarded him gravely. "Did you find Lord Atwater?"

"Led me on a merry chase all day." Trey took another cake. "Chin up, girl. I'm going to collar him at the assembly tonight. I confirmed with his clerk he'll be there. He won't directly refuse to have a word with me."

"That's all very well, but what if he doesn't have any intelligence? It's a slim hope to begin with, and—" Arabella bit down the words *your supervisor is going to make you exorcise me tomorrow morning*. She finished softly with, "I don't have much time left."

"That's why pursuing Atwater isn't my only option. I asked Halford to trace your ring, and I've got a couple of my own spells searching at the same time."

He noted Arabella's frown and explained, "Halford was the previous supervisor of the Bureau. I had to bring him into it. Winter had me looking for phantasms along the procession route all afternoon."

"Oh." Arabella found that she was rubbing her hands together nervously. "Trey…" *What will you do if it's too late to return me to my body? Would you really banish me? Do I want you to be the one to do it? Or would I rather someone else did?*

His look was narrow-eyed, sharp. "What is it?"

She couldn't ask after all. Arabella hunched her shoulders and confessed, "I, um, went into your library. I saw… the book."

Trey didn't ask which book. "And?" He had an odd, questioning expression on his face.

"It was horrible." Arabella shuddered at the memory. "It seemed to be leaking evil."

"Fascinating." Trey looked at her as if she were an interesting specimen. "Most people feel nothing more than a vague sense of discomfort, if that."

"I don't see how *anyone* can bear to be in the same room as that book," Arabella burst out.

"Meaning you're wondering what sort of morals I have, to keep it around." Trey gave a short laugh, devoid of mirth. He pushed his hands in his pockets. "I take no pleasure in it, I assure you. It's there as a reminder."

Of what? she wondered. His expression, shuttered and frowning, didn't invite further probing. Arabella squared her shoulders. "I think I should be at the Spring Assembly tonight. If I saw Lord Atwater, I might remember something."

His brow cleared. "I planned to bring you anyway. There's someone I want you to meet."

"Who?" asked Arabella, just as a bell rang.

Trey turned away. "That'd be my cousin's valet. Whit sends him over to make me presentable for every important social occasion, so I don't disgrace the family."

"Whit?" Arabella's brow furrowed. Realization and awe dawned over her. "You mean to say *Beau Whitfield* is your cousin?"

"Deplorable, isn't it?" said Trey cheerfully. "Hardly a connection to boast about."

"I'd say it was Mr. Whitfield who has more cause for bemoaning his relations," Arabella shot back.

Grinning, Trey raised a hand in acknowledgment of the hit. "Best get in the cellar, Bella. Briggs is as mundane as they come, but I'd rather not take any chances."

"Why, Lord St. Ash. To think you care so much." Arabella fluttered her eyelashes at him. Before he could respond, she let herself fall through the floor and into the cellar.

Chapter Eight

THE HORSE SNORTED AND PAWED the ground as Trey put his foot on the carriage step. The driver called out to the creature, "Wot's gotten into you, beastie? Settle down, boy." Despite the roughness of his tone, his words were gentle. The horse tossed its head once, eyes rolling and unhappy, but stood still.

"Sorry," called Trey. "Must smell the Quadrangle on me." He ducked into the hackney before the driver could respond.

Arabella, pale and glimmering, seated as far away from the horse as she could get, gave him a wan smile. The horse ceased objecting to her presence, and broke into a brisk, bone-jarring trot. Trey held onto the strap, while Arabella, sitting demurely, hands in her lap and ankles crossed, sank and rose in the seat.

Trey searched her solemn expression. "It happens sometimes, when animals sense spirits. Don't worry about it."

"I'm not," she said with a kind of tragic dignity. "I'm thinking of… other things." She raised her chin, as if defying Trey to just try and console her.

He smothered a smile before it could even twitch his lips. "Then accept my apologies for my presumption."

She gave him a regal nod and transferred her gaze to the window. Newfangled gas lights illuminated the way.

Trey could read the tension in her very posture. There was a kind of determined courage in her eyes.

She hadn't been wrong about the time left to her. And Trey couldn't offer her false assurances. It wasn't in his nature to do so—and he thought too highly of her to be dishonest about her chances. Arabella was no fragile flower.

Still, thought Trey, turning his head to glare into the gloom outside, he would do everything in his power to run Lord Atwater to ground tonight. That sharp, shivery feeling inside of him, the one he thought of as his intuition, told him that Atwater was connected to the whole reeking business.

His mother had taught him to pay attention to that feeling. After all, he'd inherited it from her.

The hackney slowed as it entered a crowded street sparkling with light, from the orange and yellow flickers of torches to the cool steady glow of rune lanterns in jewel colors. Carriages, hackneys, and chairs milled in confusion; drivers and coachmen and servants cried out to make way for Duke this and Lady that.

"We're here." Trey looked at Arabella questioningly. "Shall we alight?"

Arabella nodded. "Yes, please."

"Stay close to me, then. I've put a charm on you that should keep anyone else from seeing you, but it'd be better for you to keep out of Winter's sight. When we get in, I want you to go straight into the Lilac Room. You remember where it is?"

"Up the stairs, to the left, third door on the right," she recited his instructions from earlier. "Who am I supposed to meet? You never said."

"That's right, I didn't. And I'm not going to tell you, either." At her look, he said, "I don't want you to go into this meeting with any preconceived ideas."

"You're not setting up an appointment with anyone else from the Phantasm Bureau, are you?" Arabella asked in tones of great suspicion.

"Certainly not." Trey rapped on the roof of the hackney. The carriage came to a stop, and he opened the door and jumped out. "Come on."

He didn't wait for her. It would look decidedly odd for him to hold the door open for an invisible lady. Trey flipped a gold coin to the driver for his trouble—that sweating, shivering horse needed a hot mash and clean straw more than anything else this evening—and joined a throng of pedestrians streaming up to the marble steps of Merrimack's. Light blazed from every window, the seething murmur of vast crowds surged into the night. The columns of the portico were festooned with climbing plants, delicate blossoms glowing in rainbow colors. The carved reliefs on the pediment appeared to be in motion, acting out the well-known story of Astrid Hildottir befriending the pegasus Windswift.

Beside him, Arabella gasped at the sight of the edifice. Trey glanced down at her and saw her face lit up with delight. Gone were the dark doubts; she looked about with a frank wonder that the jaded would call gauche.

Well, none of them could see her now. She'd be able to enjoy the spectacle untroubled by their sneers. As well she should. He felt suddenly and fiercely protective of her joy.

Arabella looked at him and said gently, "I know that you're here on business matters, Trey, but it *is* the Spring Assembly."

He realized he was scowling at the mental image of bored society leaders looking down on his companion and instantly smoothed his brow. "You're right, of course. Notice the undines in the fountains." He nodded towards streams of water that arced into the sky, then formed into mist-masted ships sailing on a river of minute stars under a perfect, transparent moon.

A younger couple Trey barely knew gave him an odd look as they passed by. Trey bowed to them, and they responded with stiff bows of their own. From their expressions, Trey knew he had added to his reputation for strangeness.

It didn't bother him. His family was known for being peculiar. And eccentricity had its uses.

He detached Arabella from the spectacle of the water elementals by moving on. She hurried to keep up, but her face was still turned towards the show as a multitude of fluid mermaids and fish, each tiny form perfect in detail, slapped their tails. Diamond droplets fell over a group of women. The ladies cried out in dismay and scurried away from the splashing.

Arabella giggled at this, and one of the undines, shaped into a sea horse, floated over and playfully batted her transparent cheek.

"And they're a mischievous lot, too," remarked Trey to no one in particular, "who don't need the added encouragement."

They joined the crush of people at the entrance. Arabella, forced between two slender columns, tipped her head up to where a multitude of sparks, the lowliest of the fire elementals, barely more than specks of light, moved in mesmerizing patterns.

Mesmerizing to those who paid attention, that is. All around Trey, peers greeted each other, complained about the crowd, and declared they were dying of thirst. A plump matron in purple gauze and a feathered turban caught Trey's eye and smiled invitingly.

It took him a moment to extract the woman's name from his memory. "How do you do, Mrs. Price?" He bowed, thankful the crush precluded him from taking the lady's hand.

"Ah, Lord St. Ash, I feel quite faint already!" The woman fanned herself vigorously, but her bright eyes and red cheeks belied her claims. "Oh, did you ever *see* such a headpiece?"

Trey had no need to look over his shoulder to know who she was talking about. There was only one person who delighted in amazing and shocking the *ton* with her sense of fashion. "Don't worry, ma'am. I have it on good authority that the creature on Lady Grafton's head is, in fact, quite dead."

He felt Barbara's glare between his shoulder blades and knew he'd have to pay penance for the remark soon enough.

It had been worth it, though. Mrs. Price's eyes rounded to hear him tease such an important personage as the Countess Grafton. But then, to Trey, Barbara was only his cousin.

There had to be some advantage, no matter how small, to being related to such vast numbers of the peerage.

"Oh, but I believe you are acquainted with my daughter, Priscilla. My love," Mrs. Price took the arm of the tall, slender girl next to her, "here is Lord St. Ash." She added, confidingly, "It is only because of Priscilla I am here at all. She must come to this assembly, and no wonder, for young girls are so energetic these days. Whereas I would be perfectly content to be at home with a book. Is that not so, Priscilla?"

"Indeed, Mama," said the girl with a distinct lack of enthusiasm. From her expression, she was already heartily bored, but a speculative interest kindled in her blue eyes as she surveyed Trey. "How do you do, my lord?" There was a subtle emphasis on the *lord*.

Trey's smile, already fake, froze. As a plain Mister he had often been overlooked. But now he bore Damien's title, and it wasn't the first time previously uninterested parties looked at him in a matchmaking light. He gave a polite reply and ignored the sight of Arabella making faces at Miss Price.

Miss Price made a number of remarks in a grave tone at odds with their superficial content. Trey responded with noncommittal noises, while the translucent Arabella copied Miss Price's languid hand gestures and struck the poses the blond was known for.

Abominable girl, he thought, trying not to laugh.

The line moved. Finally, Trey saw the doorman inspecting vouchers at the entrance. Grimm, the neatly-dressed gnome who managed Merrimack's under the aegis of its patronesses, stood next to the liveried muscle, hands behind his back, shrewd black eyes missing nothing.

He nodded at Trey. "Pleasant evening to you, Lord St. Ash." His voice was deep and gravelly, in contrast to his small stature.

That was all the admittance he needed. Trey didn't even have to make a show of searching for the card he'd misplaced weeks ago; he strolled right in, while less exalted persons clutched their own gilt-edged vouchers and watched enviously.

There was a glimmer next to him, tingling against his skin. Arabella pressed close as they entered the foyer, flooded with light, reeking of perfume, and amplifying tenfold the chatter and rustle of the highborn.

Wards crackled against his skin. Trey noted the runes worked into the gilt decorations and brocade wall-hangings. Mirrors set into the ceiling duplicated the chamber below, one triangular section at a time.

Mirrors were used in powerful magic, both white and black. They could also show the unseen. Trey's eyes narrowed and he glanced at Arabella. She had gone so transparent, he could barely make out her form. Only her eyes were dark and wide, like holes into the Shadow Lands.

She noticed him looking and offered a slight smile. Her eyes were normal, and he shook his head to clear away the unnerving fancy.

Divested off his outerwear by Grimm's efficient underlings, Trey joined a short queue to greet one of Merrimack's influential patronesses. Lady Kirkland raised her thin eyebrows at him. "This is unexpected," she said bluntly, as he bowed.

"According to my family, I have obligations." Trey felt no need to pretend pleasure. Lady Kirkland's hawkish features and no-nonsense style had earned her a reputation for disagreeableness, but Trey preferred her to the other patronesses. She didn't expect him to charm or flirt, nor was she fazed by his occasional brusqueness.

"Since when have those been a concern to you? Still, seeing you here will be heartening. You know how nervous people are before Holy Week."

"Much as I'm flattered by this assessment," said Trey, "you'd be far better off breaking those mirrors." He nodded towards the offending decorations. "It wasn't so long ago that you had to have special permission to own one—and for good reason."

"I know." Lady Kirkland's lips puckered. "But I was outnumbered by the others." She shrugged her bony shoulders.

Her mother, Trey recalled, had been from Ruthenia, that vast snow-bound country to the west, poised over Vaeland like a glittering wave in a slate-grey sea. Ruthenia revered their phantasmists, understandably so. Lady Kirkland would know the stories. She and the Viscount St. Ash were only acquaintances, but in some small way, they understood each other.

"Keep trying," he advised her. "You may use my name." He grinned. "Though that may have the opposite effect."

She snorted. "It probably will." And with that, Lady Kirkland turned to the next guest. Trey strolled away, Arabella full of suppressed questions beside him. In the light, she was so faint he was afraid he'd lose sight of her. Two ladies passed by; Trey tugged Arabella's arm to prevent a dance card from slicing through her back.

There were too many people here, and anyone could have a touch of the sight, amplified by those blasted mirrors. Fortunately, good manners required elementalists to leave their companions at home. "Go to the Lilac Room and wait there," he told Arabella.

She nodded, but before she could speak, a voice, speaking in a rich drawl called out, "There you are, Trey, old fellow."

At over six feet, Beau Whitfield stood out above the crowd. In his inimitable way, he had cleared the space around him. There was no chance of anyone stumbling into him and wrinkling *his* coat or spilling claret on his snowy-white stockings.

"Go," Trey muttered to Arabella and gave his cousin a rueful smile that acknowledged the other's magnetism. Whit might be a leader of fashion, with his exquisitely-arranged cravat and elegant clothing, but he was also a fine sportsman. His coat was molded to his broad shoulders, showing off an excellent physique.

Whit had always been poised and well-dressed, much to the chagrin of his sister Barbara. Perhaps her outlandish attire, in part, was a rebellion against her older brother's effortless charm.

Whit examined his cousin rather more critically. "You'll do," he finally said.

"It was your man, after all," Trey pointed out.

"Indeed. How much did you make Briggs cry this time?"

"Only about a pint. I was in a tractable mood." Trey watched Arabella's ghostly form flit through the foyer and into the dancing room. He frowned, but he could hardly call out to her.

She probably just wanted a look. It'd be her bad luck—and his—if she happened to run into Winter.

Whit was still talking, but Trey missed most of it. "What?"

Whit followed Trey's look. "Didn't think she was your type, coz." It took Trey a moment to register that the languid Miss Price, dressed in white, had entered the dancing room after Arabella.

"She isn't," he said shortly. "What about my father?"

"*I asked* if my esteemed uncle would be here tonight," said Whit, with no ironic inflection on the esteemed bit.

"How should I know?" said Trey.

"He is your father," Whit explained with exaggerated patience.

"I'm not in my father's counsels. I'd be surprised if he were here. He doesn't come to Lumen much anymore."

"And you avoid going home to Whitecross," said Whit. His tone was neutral, but it still grated.

"I'm not a gentleman of leisure, Whit. I work here." Trey's eyebrows drew together as he gave the Beau a suspicious look. "Why the sudden interest in my relationship with my father?"

"I think," said Whit somberly, "your family's been fractured too much already for the two of you to be at such odds."

"We aren't at odds, Whit. Rest assured that my sire and I get along very well indeed—at a distance." This state of affairs was nothing new. For as long as Trey could remember it had always been him and his mother, and Damien and his father. It was the way their magical gifts had manifested. Damien had inherited their father's ferromental ability, while Trey took after their mother. All his life, Trey had felt a vague, unvoiced disapproval from his father, as if a Shield had no business dabbling in the things of the Shadow Lands.

It had only grown after what happened to his mother. Both had been relieved when Trey went off to Holyrood.

But now was no time to dredge up the past, no matter what Whit thought. He had other things to do. "Is the Duchess here yet?" he asked.

"Haven't seen her. I was told her health was too poor for her to attend."

Trey twitched his shoulder. "That's what they always say, to keep her from being mobbed." He felt restless. "I'd better go find her."

"Still working, I see." Whit shook his head. "All you Shields are the same. Thank the saints I wasn't born one."

"I'll drink to that," said Trey amiably. "Because then I'd have to own you as a brother. Later, Whit."

He stepped toward the dancing room, not because he expected the Duchess to be there, but to give a certain irrepressible ghost a stern frown and send her packing to the Lilac Room.

A familiar voice, rich and plummy and full of promises, caught his ear.

Atwater, in the middle of a group of cronies, was entering the card rooms.

Trey turned abruptly, making the lady behind him squeal in surprise. He neatly avoided a collision and threw a perfunctory apology over his shoulder. His eyes never left his target.

I'm not letting you get away this time, Atwater. Arabella's life depends on what you may know.

Chapter Nine

THE INNER ROOMS OF MERRIMACK'S were even more crowded than the foyer had been. And, of course, no one made space for a ghost. Arabella found herself pushed into pillars and tangled with draperies. At one point, a rotund red-faced gentleman swung his arm, hand holding a glass of wine, right through her.

"S-sorry!" squeaked Arabella, eyes wide as she stared at the blue-clad limb in her torso.

Of course he didn't hear her. The gentleman completed his gesture and moved on, leaving Arabella feeling rather shaken. It was decidedly odd, being impaled by an arm and a goblet.

She skittered onto the dance floor. The musicians played a stately quadrille, the strings straining to be heard above the ocean-murmur of so many voices.

Arabella wove among the dancers, walking on tip toes, trying to spot someone she knew. A statuesque brunette in grey silk clipped Arabella's ankle with a swirl of her skirt. The touch was slight and cool and mildly ticklish. Arabella could only be grateful that voluminous hooped skirts and towering wigs had gone out of fashion.

She had fancied she had a decent-sized acquaintance in Lumen. Now, looking at the indifferent, unseeing faces of the *ton*, she realized just how few she knew. So these were all the people who had spent the last months at house parties and on lavish estates. Now they were back in town for the Vernal Rites. And the Season wasn't even in full swing yet!

Arabella sidestepped a youth clearly concentrating on his steps and scanned the faces at the far wall. She didn't expect to see dear Aunt Cecilia or her cousin Harry among them. Guilt throbbed in her chest—her own impetuous foolishness had given her kind relatives such grief and robbed them of their peace of mind.

Oh, but Charlotte and Viola were both here. Buoyed again, Arabella hastened towards her friends and stood beaming down at them. "Here you are!" she said merrily. "I know you can't see me at all, but I'm with you in spirit. Despite what happened, I truly wish you would enjoy yourselves…" She faltered as she looked at their faces.

Charlotte's expression was decidedly brooding, her usually laughing rosebud mouth thin and compressed. Her gloved hands were clenched in the pink skirts of the beaded gown she had coaxed out of her fond parents. Viola beside her looked more composed, but was paler than normal in blue satin edged with gold. She sat straight with her hands folded on her lap, but her lines were stiff.

Powder could not quite hide the shadows under their eyes.

"Oh, but you mustn't distress yourselves so!" cried Arabella, distressed herself. "I'll be back to myself tomorrow, and we shall all have a good cry and a good laugh over pastries and ice cream at Hunter's."

Neither girl's expression changed, though Charlotte twitched a shoulder impatiently. Her brown ringlets brushed against her smooth, caramel-kissed skin.

"Do get up and dance! Charlotte, weren't you looking forward to flirting with Lord Ellington?" Both of their dance cards were empty.

Charlotte's eyes narrowed. She tilted her head slightly, as if a whisper tickled the edge of her hearing. Arabella focused her imploring attention on her friend, willing Charlotte to be her normal self.

To her horror, a tear appeared at the corner of Charlotte's eye.

"Courage, Charlotte," said Viola, not taking her gaze off the dance floor.

"I'm fine," said Charlotte stoutly. "It's just that Arabella would've loved to be here. She'd be so amazed at everything, the silly goose, like a child at the Amphitheater. I know I always tease her for being rustic, but it's so much fun to watch her expressions. It's all wrong that she's not..." Her voice broke.

Arabella, struck silent, pressed her hands together, caught between two impulses. She didn't know whether to rush and embrace her friends or tiptoe away and leave them to their sadness. It seemed all wrong to be privy to these confessions from Charlotte, who she'd always thought of as rather worldly and jaded.

"Dissolving into tears won't help Arabella any," said Viola, still with that distant calm. "Just bear it, Charlotte." The words appeared cold, but Arabella could see the trouble in Lady Stanhope's sea-green eyes.

"No, they won't," agreed Charlotte with a little laugh, dashing the tear away. "But Trey Shield can. And he'd better," she continued fiercely, "or else I shall put toads in his bed and honey in his shoes the next time he visits!"

Arabella couldn't help a watery chuckle of her own at these dire threats. "He will, Charlotte," she assured her friend. "I trust him." Right then, she believed the words implicitly. "And then you shall tell me why he calls you Charlie and what other pranks you've played on him."

Miss Price glided past, casting a glance at Charlotte and Viola. She remarked to her partner, rather loudly, "I do not know why *some* people would come to an assembly if they were going to insist on looking like mourners at a funeral, do you?"

Charlotte's eyes kindled. "Shrew," she muttered. Viola shot her a reproving look that failed to quench her, while Arabella choked back a giggle.

She leaned over Charlotte and said, "You are a dear friend, and I hope to have many opportunities to tell you so." She gently straightened the silk flower tucked behind Charlotte's ear and floated away.

Behind her, Charlotte exclaimed, "Viola!"

"What is it?"

"Did you hear that?"

"Hear what?"

Charlotte's voice dropped. "A kind whisper on a small, perfumed wind."

Arabella smiled to herself and whisked into a supper room where, she had been told repeatedly, she would see culinary masterpieces designed to delight the senses.

Her aunt and friends had not exaggerated the gastronomical excesses of the Spring Assembly. Rows of silver chafing dishes, each covered with a silver lid engraved with Merrimack's name, stood on a sideboard. Pyramids of fruit and statues of pastry reigned in an opposite corner.

Arabella took a pinch of sugared dough from the corner of a detailed model of the Keep. The crumbs fell through her hand, leaving a sweet sticky sensation in her fingers. She stuck them in her mouth.

Her incorporeal tongue tingled, and the sensation spread through her in an odd kind of shock, like pins and needles all over her skin. For a moment, she was dizzy with the feeling, lifting dandelion-light into the air.

Get a hold of yourself. Arabella forced her aethereal body to the floor, shaken. She had been so close to spiraling completely out of control, to be blown away wherever the wind took her. She had to remember that her substance no longer obeyed the laws of nature—and that could bring her real trouble.

Arabella backed away from the desserts. The taste of human food was too strong for her. Out of her skin, she was too susceptible to what she encountered. If she wasn't careful, she might implode from the crystalline wonder of sugar.

Gnomes, short and swarthy, entered the room, carrying platters of stuffed mushrooms and fish rolls. Arabella shrank into a corner, but even the gnomes' sharp eyes couldn't make her out. While they arranged food, she slipped from the chamber and into a narrow corridor.

Servants' way, she thought as she glided through a spice-scented gloom. In the distance, strings wailed, footsteps pattered, voices bubbled. The noise was an ocean murmur in her ear, distant, removed.

The corridor stretched impossibly long ahead of her. Arabella frowned at the lack of light—the way from kitchen to supper rooms seemed like the worst place to economize.

The air took on a chilly bite, but glimmers of light, in tints of blue, illuminated the passageway. The floor underfoot changed from wooden boards to stone slabs; they struck Arabella's feet in splinters of cold. She glanced down and gasped.

Faces twisted in agony and malice slid under the surface. Their mouths opened in soundless screams. Arabella sprang back and saw that the walls, too, were no longer paneled. Instead, they were formed of half-melted stone, solidified into ripples and drips and strange curves and protrusions.

An icy shiver ran through her. The odd shapes were people, half-melted into the wall, the ripples the folds of their clothing, the curves an arched back or a bent limb.

The light sharpened, banishing some of the fuzziness, showing Arabella more detail than she wanted to see. An obsidian point of darkness lay at the end of the passageway, drawing her on.

Into the Shadow Lands.

Arabella resisted, digging in her heels. Her feet could find no purchase on the slippery floor, so she grabbed the solidified robes of a woman whose eyes held no hope. A gust of wind at her back shoved her onward.

No! It's not my time! Arabella thought fiercely of life, of hot summer days and fresh-cut hay and warm milk straight from the cow and gamboling kittens. The red chimney pots of Lumen, the reek of horse dung, the clatter of wheels on cobbled streets. Flower girls hawking their wares in thin, piercing cries; street sweepers with their long-handled brooms; ladies taking a promenade in Queens Park; elegant gentlemen riding their hacks.

She thought of Uncle Henry's mild kindliness and his old smoking jacket with the patched elbows that he wouldn't let Aunt Cecilia replace. Her aunt reclining in her morning gown, avidly devouring a romance and weeping real tears over the trials of improbably beautiful and virtuous heroines. Harry showing off fashionable clothing from a Bell Street tailor with a careless air that couldn't quite hide his excited pride.

The silk rose in Charlotte's brown hair. The curve of Viola's alabaster cheek with curls of her ash-blond hair lying against it.

Trey Shield, with narrowed eyes and distracted air, lecturing her while she secretly admired the fine figure Briggs had made of him. Really, he was quite handsome when he bothered. The long-tailed coat, grey knee-breeches, and white stockings made him look elegant—and far above her touch.

Her own body, still alive in Crescent Circle.

The alien wind, stinking of grave dirt and burning coal, buffeted her ever more fiercely. Arabella planted herself in her life, in her present joys and future hopes, and refused to give in.

She was anchored, she was weighty.

She wouldn't be blown willy-nilly into the Shadow Lands.

The wind lashed at her once more, like a tantrum-throwing child slamming the door, and died down. The stone around her misted and dissolved, leaving Arabella back in a mean corridor made of wood, smelling of old dinners and lit with oil lamps.

That dark point grew smaller, but didn't wink out. It stayed at the edge of her vision, a reminder that her victory was only temporary.

Arabella smoothed her hair and dress out of habit. Her hair lay in a thick plait down her back. She was back in one of the shapeless, homespun gowns that she had worn before Lumen, but she didn't care.

She had won back her life dressed like this. This was her triumphal garb.

She turned and plunged through a wall, hurrying for the Lilac Room.

Those brief moments in the passageway to the Shadow Lands had changed everything.

Arabella no longer retained her substance as well; she was squeezed and pinched and pulled as the crowds jostled around her. Their voices came to her from far away, as if she were underwater. The edges of her vision wavered darkly, and everything looked dull and tarnished. The light had taken on a sullen hue, the gilt on chandeliers and mirrors and ladies' dresses darkened to a dirty brass. Lines of dissipation and discontent were stark on the guests' faces.

A mournful flute, singing of regrets, rose above the musicians. The dancers on the floor moved slowly, as if through fog. Behind them, Arabella saw others—skeletons in broken crowns and moth-eaten robes, rotted corpses in scraps of silk and crawling with maggots, sharp-edged shadows she had no name for. They staggered and stumbled, swayed and slithered, parodying the moves of the mortal dancers.

Arabella veered away from the dance floor and struggled towards the foyer. Arms brushed against her, bodies bulled through her. Voices and images and desires snaked into her head. A man's thirst for wine so strong it parched her throat; a woman howling, "I'll make her pay for that, the hussy"; the creamy swell of a bosom above a beaded bodice; desire that ran like fire and grease through her soul…

Arabella half-fell into the foyer, disheveled and panting, her skirt stretched behind her in a gauzy thread, caught under someone's feet in the crush. She yanked it back to herself and gritted her teeth against the headache pounding in her temples.

All those emotions, all those thoughts. All those dark secret things laid bare in her head.

She'd lose herself in the sea of it all. Arabella took deep breaths and anchored her thoughts to a bird in lazy flight, to a boat bobbing on water, to a spider spinning her web. The repetitive motions of natural things soothed her. Gave her space in her own head to think.

She had misjudged the dangers of her situation. So what if this was Merrimack's, a place deemed safe for debutantes? So what if Trey Shield was also under this roof? So what if the wards prevented demons and corrupted spirits from entering these halls?

Arabella had nearly lost herself twice, in the Shadow Lands and among the crowds.

Gathering her skirt, Arabella silently, soberly made her way up the stairs and to the Lilac Room.

It was empty, though a fire burned in the grate. Arabella cast a desultory look around the chamber, all desire to explore completely quenched. She had passed two middle-aged gentlemen laughing together on the stairs. As they turned a corner, one had knocked into her, leaving a green smear of bitter jealousy. The other had looked at his companion and thought, his voice loud and dripping contempt in Arabella's mind, "This clumsy oaf will always fail at whatever he sets his hand to."

Their vitriol nearly sent her reeling. She'd clutched the rail, the grain scraping roughly into her sinking palms, while the two, showing each other affable masks, continued down, still chatting.

It had been a relief to see the door with *Lilac Room* etched into the brass plate. Arabella wearily pushed through the wood and circled the room, noting the writing desk laid out with fresh paper, pens, ink, and wax; a hideous urn with dog-headed demons snarling all over it; and the two stiff sofas with scroll-shaped arms. There was nothing purple nor floral about this chamber. Even the wallpaper had a maroon diamond pattern repeating endlessly across it.

Arabella threw herself into a chair by the fire. It took a little work to stay level with the seat, but once she figured the trick of it, her body stayed in place without her constantly willing it so. She huddled, with her feet up on the upholstery, her knees tucked to her chest. No one could see her to be scandalized or scold her for stretching her clothing.

Besides, ghostly wear was eminently adaptable. Her gown, cream-colored and plain, grew bigger to accommodate her unladylike position.

Arabella put her cheek in her hand and stared moodily into the fire.

More than ever, she just wanted to go *home*.

Except she couldn't figure out where home was. Was it Umbrax, with its wild seas and rocky shores and purple moors? Was it the tall house with the yellow door on Crescent Circle?

Or was it a rented row house in the City, with a pentagram in a cellar workshop, an evil book in the library, and the Shade Hunter's presence all over the place?

Arabella was so tired she couldn't summon the strength to scold herself for her fancies. The numbed feeling would've frightened her if she hadn't already felt so remote and removed from herself.

The door clicked open, then shut. Slow footsteps and the tap of a walking stick sounded on the floor. Arabella sat up as an old lady walked to the sofa and seated herself stiffly on it. Despite her age, her back was ramrod straight and the gnarled hands on the ebony-topped walking stick firm. She didn't look at Arabella, just stared into the flames.

Arabella subsided, studying the woman. Her lined face and elaborate wig were white with powder. She wore a dress that had been fashionable in her youth, with hooped skirts of green damask, an open bodice tied across a stomacher decorated with jet beads, and flounces at her elbows. A medallion of tarnished bronze on her age-spotted bosom caught the light in tiny gleams Her sunken eyes were dark and, Arabella suspected, very penetrating. An aura of authority surrounded the woman.

She was glad this grand old lady did not see her. But how was she to converse with the person Trey had wanted her to meet with this eccentric peer in the same room?

The woman said, without taking her gaze off the burning logs, "How long will you hide your gift, child?" Her voice was deeper than expected, and slightly husky.

Arabella looked around the room involuntarily, as if someone else had snuck in without her knowledge. "A-are you addressing me, Madam?" she asked timidly. How small and thin her voice sounded.

The lady turned her head slightly towards Arabella. "Who else is in the room, child?" she asked with awful patience. Arabella squirmed in her seat, remembered with horror her inelegant posture, and instantly put her feet on the floor. Too hard, for her soles sank slightly into the thin carpet. The lady went on, "I may be ancient, but I am not, as yet, in the habit of talking to myself."

A light shone in her eyes and the air in the chamber seemed to sharpen somehow, like a sword being unsheathed.

"I-I beg your pardon, ma'am," said Arabella, flushing and mortified. "I did not know I was supposed to meet you. Lord St. Ash didn't say." *As he should've!* He had sent her to meet this august personage—and this woman, whoever she was, was important and fairly crackling with power—with no preparation whatsoever.

"Ah, Trevelyan. That impossible boy, always testing the boundaries." The lady shook her head. "But we are talking of you."

"Could you—*would* you—return me to my body, ma'am?" Arabella leaned forward in her eagerness.

"I have not the power for it," said the lady simply. "I came here to see if I could enable you to do so, on your own." She looked levelly at Arabella. "You could do that, you know, if you freed your gift."

Arabella said nothing, though her hands were clenched in the translucent material of her gown.

"You don't deny it," the lady mused. "Interesting."

Arabella lifted her chin. "If you know that much, ma'am, then you must know that I cannot do as you say. You must know that the gift is"—her voice trembled—"a curse."

"I know only that it is all knotted up with pain and fear." The lady's voice was at once gentle and inexorable, like soft snow falling and falling from a winter sky. "And that you could free it, if you wished."

Arabella made a sudden, sharp gesture, as if to cut off her words. "I don't wish it. What you call a gift has left nothing but a dark taint on the earth." She strove to keep her voice from getting shrill.

The lady nodded once, slowly. "Perhaps it is too much to ask right now. After all that has happened."

"It's in the past," said Arabella firmly. She added, in a smaller voice, "Does this mean you can't help me?"

The lady frowned at the fire. "Your soul must remember again what it is like to dwell in your body. Perhaps I can assist you." Her voice dropped to a murmur. "Memory... memory is a tricky thing, like a river that rushes fast in places, meanders in others. You never know when the undercurrent will take you and pull you under. And yet, I see a place you cannot reach. A dam, blocking the river, a reservoir of memory behind it." Her brows drew together in fierce concentration.

Pressure built up in the room. Arabella held her breath. In the back of her mind, within dark recesses, impressions stirred, images flickered...

And then the feeling vanished. The memories plunged beneath the surface again. Arabella let out a soft sigh and looked expectantly at the lady.

Her mouth was set in a thin, pained line. Though she still held herself straight, she was diminished somehow, shrunken even. Under the powder, her face was grey.

"Oh, do not, madam!" Arabella sat up, alarmed. "Do not exert yourself so!" Guilt tore through her. How would she face Trey—or anyone—if something happened to this old lady on her behalf?

The woman's hands clenched around the top of her walking stick. Her head was bowed. "Once," she said, voice low and hoarse. "Once, this would've been a mere moment's work for me, a mere weaving of some threads here and unraveling of others there." She looked up and smiled without mirth at Arabella. "It is a painful thing to be old and weak."

She rose heavily to her feet, leaning on the stick. Arabella scrambled up, feeling more gauche than ever.

Even at her age, the lady was taller than Arabella. The firelight flickered over her face, kindling a spark in her dark, heavy-lidded eyes.

The room seemed to waver, as if viewed through water. The stern old lady with her erect carriage and hooped skirts was gone. In her place stood a warrior in bronze helmet and rune-etched breastplate. The folds of her once-white robe, ragged at the bottom, stained with grime, fell to her sandaled feet. In her right hand, she carried a spear tipped with starlight; in her left, a buckler that gleamed silver like the moon. Her eyes were hidden pools, dark green with shadows.

It was autumn, and a fierce sun beat upon her neck, a chill wind scraped along her face. Her feet had turned to lead, the shaft of her spear bit into her callused hand. Sorrow crept greyly over her, one thought only ringing and ringing through the fog of emotion.

He is dead. He is dead. He is dead.

Arabella jerked back, startled. She blinked, and both the image and the curious sensation of fitting into someone else's skin disappeared.

The lady cocked her head and looked on with interest. "Curious," she said. Before Arabella could respond, she reached out and brushed her fingers against Arabella's cheek.

Arabella steeled herself, but the touch was warm and pleasant.

Not so for the lady. She dropped her hand quickly, an odd expression crossing her face. Arabella could not make it out at all—mingled astonishment, pity, and… awe?

"What is it?" she whispered.

"Something I must consider on my own first," said the lady. She smiled at Arabella, wry with a touch of humor. "I apologize I could not help you. But I think you and Trevelyan can solve this on your own. Help him, child, and yourself. He risks much for you."

And with that, she left the room, her skirts rustling across the floor, the stick tip-tapping, leaving Arabella rooted to the spot.

Chapter Ten

"LORD ATWATER." TREY POSITIONED HIMSELF between the parliamentarian and the only exit out of the small room. "A word with you, if you please?"

Atwater was a man still in the prime of his life, with a full head of greying hair. His height masked his thickening girth, and his face was open and good-humored, his light blue eyes pleasant. Trey privately thought that the confidence and affability he projected had gone further in making his career than any political acumen or hard-earned wisdom.

"Ah, young Shield, is it not?" Atwater's lips curved in a ready smile, but there was no warmth in his mild eyes. "Ah, forgive me, it is Lord St. Ash now, of course."

Trey bowed stiffly, acknowledging Atwater's self-correction. "This will take but a few moments of your time, sir."

Atwater gestured around the room. "My dear young man, surely this is a night for dancing and entertaining, not business?"

"Not in my line of work," said Trey. He observed Atwater's entourage, noting how all of them were unimportant hangers-on. Surely Atwater could afford a better class of sycophants? They melted away with muttered excuses when Trey turned a cold look on them. Not nasty, just making it obvious they weren't needed. "Perhaps your clerk did not give you my messages?"

Atwater looked around the mostly-empty room. Old Lord Mosely, corpulent and gouty, snored in a chair, a handkerchief over his face. Two undistinguished men were hunched over an intense game of cribbage.

There was no one to intervene. Trey had timed his move with care. With his hand at his side where Atwater couldn't see it, he made a small gesture. The spell he had prepared sparked between his fingers and shot across the small distance between them.

"Yes, my man did say you had asked to see me," Atwater said, resigned. He wasn't smiling now; he just looked weary. "What d'you want, St. Ash?"

"This won't take long," Trey assured him. "I want to know your whereabouts Wednesday evening."

Atwater raised his eyebrows. "Am I under investigation?" he asked with surprised hauteur.

"You may have knowledge that will aid me in a disturbing case." Trey took note of Atwater's reaction, the slight tensing of his shoulders and the narrowing of his eyes.

"Well, then ask for it directly," said Atwater shortly, seeming to remember he was Trey's senior and a member of Parliament.

"I'd rather not," said Trey. His spell, a small thing of grey aether shot through with silver runes, detected no trace of the Shadow Lands on the man.

All that meant was that Atwater had had no recent direct dealings with the ghoul.

That didn't mean much. And Trey wasn't a good enough rune master to cast a halfway-reliable truth spell.

Atwater eyed him, as if wondering how much rope Trey was giving him to hang himself. Then he spread out his hands with a twitch of his shoulders. "I was in meetings at the palace late into the evening. Afterwards, I took a hackney to Green's where I had supper and met with friends. It was past midnight when I returned to my rooms. I'm sorry that I didn't think to ask the hackney driver his name, so he could corroborate my story." Sarcasm dripped from his tone.

"I have a witness," said Trey, "who spotted you in the Fleet that evening."

Atwater waved a dismissive hand. "The person was obviously under an erroneous assumption. In the twilight, anyone can mistake a superficial resemblance."

"The witness claims," Trey went on, "to have seen you coming out of a particular pawnshop. Moreover, a pawnshop whose owner was found murdered by a ghoul this morning."

"I am sorry to hear it," said Atwater, with an impatient twitch. "But I have no connection to the incident at all. You're wasting your time here, St. Ash."

"Forgive me, but I have to follow every lead. You understand."

Atwater unbent enough to bestow a small smile on Trey. "Of course," he said with a heartiness that rang false. "Your service to Vaeland is exemplary."

"Seems an unlikely connection, but I suppose I'll have to prod the accident victim, then," mused Trey, half to himself. "We'll have to bring in a better spirit seer."

Atwater's smile froze in place. For an instant, something flickered in his eyes. Then the expression was gone, and Atwater said, "You must do what you must. If you'll excuse me." He stalked off.

Trey watched Atwater leave the room, his back stiff. His spell fluttered after the politician and landed on his coat. There, it sank into the fibers and dimmed.

He'd use the aether to keep track of Atwater's movements. Trey was sure the man knew more than he'd been telling. He had not misread the fleeting emotion in the other's eyes.

It was fear.

The Duchess' message found Trey at the foot of the servants' stairway leading up to the private rooms. He'd already been accosted by Charlotte Blake, demanding to know what he was doing to help her friend, and a distant relative who'd strongly hinted that he should dance with her daughter. Trey managed to fob both women off, and escaped through the servants' corridors.

A robin, built out of intricate, interlocking runes, flew onto his shoulder. Hues of red misted into his face and the Duchess's voice rang out in his ears.

"I'm sorry, Trevelyan. I cannot unlock your friend's memories. But she may find a way to unlock them herself. I sense that this is but a ripple from something greater and more dangerous, though. Be careful."

And that was it. Trey frowned, not liking to be reminded of the Duchess's age and failing health. She'd been one of the most powerful Truth-tellers in Vaeland for decades, making her a fitting Guardian, one of the twelve magicians charged with keeping watch on the country's magical borders. Now she held her position only because they could find no one to replace her.

Due to her age, the Duchess hadn't been expected to make it to Lumen for the Vernal Rites. Trey hadn't been surprised, though, when she had put in an appearance. The Duchess had an iron will, something he'd realized when she'd been his advisor at Holyrood.

With a wry smile, Trey went in search of Arabella.

He found her outside the assembly rooms, in a small courtyard of paved stone, a quiet pond, and winter-hardy plants. The decorations here were sparse—the magic-made lights in the two stunted trees were already dying out.

She stood in one corner, head tilted up to a night sky faintly washed with stars. To his sight, she glowed with a pearly light that showed her features in fine detail—the dark arch of her eyebrows, the even white teeth biting down on her lower lip, the blush-tint of her fingernails as she clasped her hands in front of her chest.

"I never knew until now how much I missed the stars," she said as he joined her. "At night, back in Umbrax, you can see them so clearly. Here, the light and the smoke interfere with the sight."

Trey glanced at the sky. "At Whitecross Abbey, which is only twenty miles from Lumen, the view is very fine. Although I was too interested in realms other than the celestial to pay it much heed."

"Hmm. The cycles of nature rule life in Umbrax more completely than they do here," Arabella said thoughtfully. "The dance of constellations through the seasons, the waxing and waning of the moon, the rise and fall of tides. I don't even remember when the moon was last full. I used to be mindful of such things, not so long ago."

He was much more interested in her than in the moon. Had she lost substance? There was a more airy quality about her, all light and cold and aether. He felt the Shadow Lands breathing nearby, almost-doorways lurking in the dark corners of the courtyard, rippling on the pond's surface, tangled in the thin twigs of a scraggly bush.

"What are you doing out here, Arabella?" he asked, voice rougher than he intended. In her bare feet and shapeless dress, she looked different, almost fey.

"Trying to remember," she said, whisper-soft. "She said I could fish them out myself, you know. So I came here, to where it's quiet, to see what came up from the depths of memory. If there was a full moon... and if I had rosemary... that would help."

Arabella's shimmering substance spun out from the hem of her dress and from her hair hanging in a braid down her back. She was diminishing faster than he had expected, as if bringing her here had only hastened the process.

The only things he could do to stop her decline were all against the rules—not Winter's fussy regulations, but the laws set down by others like him throughout Vaeland's history.

He had been a thoughtless idiot and flouted them once. He knew better now.

But still. Trey looked into Arabella's distant eyes and pale face and couldn't let her go without a fight.

Music drifted through the long glass windows—a waltz just striking up.

"Shall we dance?" He held out his hand to her.

Arabella's smile was slight, but the amusement kindling in her eyes made her look more like her old self. "I'm not as gauche as all that, sir. I haven't been given permission to dance the waltz by the patronesses."

"They'll never know." Still, he held out his hand, and she laid her own on it. Her fingers were cold and fragile in his clasp, as if they would dissolve to mist at the merest pressure. He guided her out to a clear space in the courtyard. Her dress changed as he did so, becoming something more in fashion, but in the hues of the night sky, blues and silvers bleeding into each other across the folds. The bodice was sprinkled with a thousand points of light, like miniature stars. Some burned white, others tinted blue and red.

She had no idea, he thought, that she was doing this. What had the Duchess said? Arabella Trent could unlock her own memories. She must have some sort of gift or fey blood in her, if even half the stories he'd heard about Umbrax were true.

"You will look very odd, dancing by yourself, if someone should chance to come onto the balcony and look down," Arabella remarked as they faced each other, his arm around her waist, her midnight-gloved hand in his. He was heartened by the laughter in her face. Even her voice, with that edge of teasing, sounded like the Arabella he knew.

But then, was the Arabella he knew the real one?

"I shall risk it," said Trey, pushing his fancies away. "If nothing else, it will add to my reputation for eccentricity, which is to my advantage. I could do with fewer invitations to supper parties."

"And fewer chances of being cornered by determined misses ready to extract your guineas for worthy causes." She dimpled at him, following his lead with an easy grace.

"Exactly." He grinned at her. Arabella seemed embarrassed, for she dropped her gaze to stare studiously at his cravat which, he knew, was well-tied for once. "You dance very well," he said to the top of her dark head, her hair now coiled up and threaded through with a silvery headpiece, delicately formed into the shape of some creeping plant.

Again that flash of a pleased smile. "Oh, no. I've had lessons for months with Charlotte, and I'm convinced the dancing master thinks I'm as clumsy as an ox in a buttercup field."

"Man has no idea what he's talking about." Trey twirled her around with expert ease. She followed his lead, her face aglow. "I expect he's old and crotchety and bandy-legged."

"With a wrinkled neck like a chicken's," Arabella confided. "I'm persuaded that only the crossest and ugliest men are deemed suitable dancing masters for young ladies."

"But, of course. You can't have the daughters of peers running off with their dashing dancing masters. Something about the music and the movement tends to addle the brain and makes one more susceptible to attachment."

Her feet faltered for a moment, but Arabella recovered quickly. "How absurd, sir. I imagine that hundreds of ladies and gentlemen dance together without the least danger of falling in love."

"Indeed. That has been my personal experience," said Trey. He felt her shift away from him and berated himself for leading them into this perilous conversational thread. She had so few friends at the moment; she didn't need to worry if he had designs on her. The notion was ridiculous. "You, I'm sure, are far too sensible to do so."

She inclined her head in gracious acceptance, but she had gone remote again, her gaze beyond his shoulder and her head tilted as if listening to distant music.

Music.

Saints!

Realization struck him with the force of a blow.

He'd been so focused on putting Arabella at ease, at striving to be pleasant and sociable, that he'd missed the Shadow Lands creeping into the scene. The music had changed from the sprightly waltz to something slower, melancholy, haunting. A pipe, carved from the thigh bone of a murdered child, raised its voice in lament, while strings twisted from the hair of drowned maidens carried on a sobbing counterpoint.

And he himself had slowed, matching his steps to the otherworldly tune, drawing himself and Arabella into the web spun by that eerie place. Already it gathered around her, changing the angle of the light and casting odd shadows that shouldn't have been there.

Without thinking, he tightened his grip and pulled her closer. She felt light and delicate as a sparrow, as if at any moment she would fly away—or snap.

Trey forced himself to think of an earthly tune, repeating the melody in his own head, drowning out the phantasmal song with his own voice. Ta da da *da*. Ta da da *da* da *dum*. His feet seemed to be stuck in mud, they were so slow to follow his lead. Trey looked down at Arabella, at her dark hair like shadows in a midnight forest, her substance thin and translucent like porcelain.

Her entire body strained to follow that other music. She lagged, resisting his hold. "Arabella," he said, through teeth gritted with the effort of keeping them back from that hungry maw, "I'm leading, not you."

Awareness dawned on her face, mingled with horror. She started to turn her head—he had no idea what she saw—but he said roughly, "No! Don't give it your attention. Keep your eyes on me." Obediently, she stared up at him, her expression fixed and scared and intent. He saw the flicker of her eyes as her look strayed to the sides, saw her struggle to keep her gaze on him.

"Good girl. Now, mind, follow me. Focus on my face, my voice, my steps." Trey hummed the melody, moving out of the pattern, dragging Arabella with him. He felt her tension; she wanted both to stay and to go. He thought, *Its call grows stronger.*

But, grim and determined, Trey took them both back out, retracing the careless path that had brought them into peril. The other realm's hold loosened. Another step, a final effort, a last jolt. With a pop, the Shadow Lands let them go.

They were back in the courtyard of Merrimack's, the waltz washing over them as if a soap bubble of silence had burst. The lights from the windows were at a full cheerful blaze, and the shrubbery was just as meager and sad as before. Trey was out of breath, as if he'd run a mile, and there was a quivering ache in his muscles. He gripped Arabella by the shoulders; she was pressed up to his chest.

"Hey." He gave her a little shake. "Are you all right?"

Arabella gave a little sigh and snuggled closer. She said, voice small and muffled, "It's so cold, Trey. So cold. I feel the wind blowing right through me. I'm so cold, and you're so warm."

A frisson ran like fire through his nerves. Memories flashed through his mind.

Celeste's lovely voice, throbbing and broken-hearted, saying, "Warm me up, my love"... Damien pulling her close... Her shudder of relief, and then her head turning, fangs flashing, teeth sinking into his brother's neck... Damien's warm red blood spurting...

Trey pushed Arabella away from him, his fingers clenching on her shoulders. His wards buzzed, and Arabella flinched. "Ow!"

The hurt look she turned on him was completely human. Her eyes didn't turn red, her mouth didn't split open into a maw, she didn't wail or attack him with suddenly-extended claws.

"Sorry," said Trey. "But remember you're a ghost and your substance yearns for a body. And you can't have mine."

"I have a perfectly nice one of my own, thank you," said Arabella indignantly. "I don't want yours."

He grinned at her. "That sounds naughty, Miss Trent."

It still amused him that a ghost could flush, and in spectacular fashion. Her cheeks flooded with pink. "It's only naughty if you take it that way," she told him, trying for frostiness but failing.

"I've been told before that I'm an indelicate boor," said Trey. "You won't have to put up with it too much longer."

The color in her cheeks subsided. "I have to thank you once more." She started to look over her shoulder, then checked herself. "The... the other realm was very near."

"It was my fault. I should've been more careful."

"Who was she?" Her expression was solemn.

"What?"

"The woman in your memory just now," said Arabella. "The one who turned."

His jaw tightened. So she had seen that, had she? The boundaries—between worlds, between bodies—were indeed blurring for her.

That wasn't good.

Never you mind. He opened his mouth to say just those words. But what came out, slightly hoarse and stumbling, was, "Her name was Celeste. She was my brother's wife."

"So the man was…?"

"Damien, yes. My brother." His hands clenched by his sides, the old wound aching once more. It would never completely heal; there would always be the scar and the occasional flash of pain to remind him it was there.

"I'm sorry." Her compassion was deep and sincere. And she didn't follow up with prying questions. She stood there, accepting the burden of his loss, offering nothing but sympathy, asking for nothing more than he was ready to give.

Trey went on, the words tumbling over themselves. "She wasn't gifted… no, that's all wrong, to talk of Celeste as if she were merely ordinary. She was gifted, but not with magic. She had the voice of an angel and a beauty that was hard to grasp." He shook his head, unable to express with mere words what Celeste had been like. "And she carried within her a well of deep joy and warmth. My brother loved her and she him. He was a Shield and a darn good elementalist, so everyone thought she'd be safe. But they got to her during the Incursion, regardless, and through her to him. And so it ended, the way you saw."

It was the first time he had spoken of this. The first time he'd told this sad tale to anyone in full.

Arabella made a gesture with her cupped hands, as if accepting the words. Accepting his trust.

"It's not a mistake I care to repeat," said Trey, kicking a pebble. It skittered across the courtyard.

"Do you really think," she asked, "that your brother's marriage was a mistake?"

He thought about it, really thought about it. After the Incursion, the shocked and sorrowful gifted had whispered words to the effect. *She wasn't strong and was thus targeted. Magic and mundane should not mix.* Back then, he might've agreed. But now?

"No. They were happy together. Who am I to begrudge them that?"

Damien hadn't. He had died with his wife in his arms, smiling as her tears mingled with his blood.

"You loved her." It was not a question.

"She was my sister."

"Not quite like that." Arabella's smile was knowing, but gentle. Perceptive once again, she'd seen something no else had ever known.

He found that he didn't mind much at all. If someone had to glean it, he'd rather it was Arabella. "Maybe not. But I loved my brother far more and would never hurt him." Trey folded his arms. "Any more questions, Miss Curious?"

The heavy sarcasm in his voice didn't faze her one bit. "One more." She blithely ignored his frown. "*What* incursion? Despite the troubles on the continent, Vaeland hasn't been invaded since before I was born."

Trey considered her expression of friendly curiosity. Then he sighed. She'd already experienced more of the Shadow Lands that most people, gifted or not, did. He'd let slip the word, so he might as well tell her, before she went ferreting out the information on her own and got all the wrong ideas.

"You know the Shadow Lands attempt to break into the mortal realms. Sometimes they succeed."

Arabella shivered. "I thought the Guardians and the Regalia and the Vernal Rites prevented that."

"They do. Mostly. But sometimes it's not enough. Like the Great Incursion last year."

Her eyebrows drew together. "What did you call it?"

"The Great Incursion. It's a silly name, but—" He stopped.

Arabella wasn't listening. Her eyes had gone wide. "I've heard the name before," she breathed. "In Mr. Gibbs's shop. When I went in, he was talking to someone in the back room and I heard them say the name. And-" She squeaked. "Trey!"

The portal snapped open so suddenly that Trey had no warning. It glared like a dragon's eye and inhaled like a dragon's maw. Tendrils of flame grabbed Arabella around the waist and arms. She cried out as they dragged her back, her hands reaching desperately out for him.

"Arabella!" He leapt forward, hands outstretched. Her ghostly fingers brushed his as the portal closed around her. The last thing he saw was her white face and her lips moving, saying, "Trey, it was *miasma!*" as the rent snapped shut.

Damn it! Trey could still feel her, on the other side of the boundary. He'd summon Sorrow and cut his way through to her—

He couldn't lift his arm. His feet were frozen to the ground. Startled, Trey looked down. Chains of silver runes, each one precise and elegant and strong as iron, bound him fast.

Winter's spellwork.

He couldn't materialize Sorrow properly with the runes interfering. She misted into his hand, her edges blurred. He slashed down at the spell, runes crumpling under his blade, Sorrow gaining definition with every stroke. Yet still more chains spiraled around him, tethering him to the mortal plane.

Arabella was getting further and further away from him. "Winter, let go!" he ground out through clenched teeth.

The man himself stood at the edge of the courtyard, his arms raised in arcane gestures. His usually impeccable clothes were rumpled. Sweat sheened his face as Trey strained his spell to a breaking point.

There. The Shadow Lands were right there, within reach. Binding runes tightened around Trey, and Sorrow flared in response. They melted into quicksilver droplets, dissolving into the night.

Trey slashed a rip in the air, creating an opening. The Shadow Lands glimmered beyond it.

He could sense Arabella's presence as a fast-fading trail of blue. He was almost there.

Sorrow misted, her light dying. The edges of the portal turned to sludge. The rip inched shut, bit by bit. More chains weighed him down, bindings dragged him away.

A rough-edged baritone rose up in a half-song, half-chant. The others were here. Trey recognized their magic before he even made out their forms. Morgan, Lee, even Sutton. All of them holding him back.

They couldn't keep him indefinitely, but they didn't have to.

Arabella was gone. That gleaming trail through the Shadow Lands disappeared.

A ghost like her, with no hunger or rage, would leave little trace.

Trey pushed back against the spellwork holding him. Winter's chains slipped off as August dropped his arms tiredly. Morgan staggered and Sutton fell onto his rump.

Free at last, Trey stalked up to Winter, Sorrow whole and solid in his hand. "What the hell did you do that for?" he snarled.

Winter looked at him, face pinched and grey, a tightness Trey could not decipher around his mouth. "What am I to say to your father," he said with awful gentleness, "if he lost you to the Shadow Lands, too?"

Chapter Eleven

TREY PROPPED UP A WALL in Winter's office, staring at Atwater through narrowed eyes. The politician, looking shrunken and tired, sagged in a chair and ran his hands through his thick mane.

"So, yes, I was at that pawnshop. I admit that—and I also lied to St. Ash about it. Truth is, my election campaign is costing me money I don't have. So I've been pawning some of my personal effects."

Winter stood, leaning his hands on his desk. In front of him was a statement from Atwater's clerk confirming that the politician had slipped out between meetings Wednesday evening. Sutton had divined the whereabouts of the hackney driver that had taken Atwater to the Fleet—not hard to do considering the man was in the hospice, reeking of phantasmia, magic of the Shadow Lands far more inimical to mortal life than the aether Trey used in Vaeland. The driver remembered taking up a gentleman, but nothing much after that. He had been found in the wreckage of his own carriage in a field outside Lumen, his horse screaming in pain, leg broken.

Lee reported that the wreckage was riddled with phantasmia and rotting quickly. The horse, crazed and sprouting horns and drooling poison, had to be put down.

Trey was sure this was the carriage that had run Arabella Trent down in the street on her way home Wednesday night. That Atwater was also connected to it was no coincidence.

Arabella. His hand clenched. It had been four hours since her disappearance. The Phantasm Bureau had been busy in that time, but it wasn't enough.

It was almost Saturday.

Winter levelled a penetrating look at Atwater. "Why in the Fleet, though? There are more respectable money lenders elsewhere."

"Because, August," said Atwater, with a hint of acerbity in his voice, "I was embarrassed. I didn't want anyone to know I was purse-pinched. I went to the Fleet, so no one would recognize me." He gave a short bark of laughter, entirely without humor. "It didn't work."

"And why that pawnshop?" August persisted.

Atwater shrugged impatiently, as if twitching off an annoying fly. "Because it was deep in the Fleet and looked as if it would be able to preserve my anonymity."

"You mean it looked secretive and shady." Trey spoke for the first time.

Atwater turned his head. The two exchanged looks, Atwater angry, nostrils flared; Trey cold and hard.

Atwater dropped his stare first. "Yes, I suspected some petty criminal activity was going on. After all, it's the Fleet. But it's been tolerated for as long as Lumen has existed. How was I supposed to know Gibbs dealt in contraband from his back room? He didn't offer me a jar of kraken's blood in exchange for my pocket watch!"

"Saints, Reginald!" Winter shook his head. "If you were having trouble, you should've come to your friends first."

"Friends, August?" Atwater's smile was bitter. Now that he'd dropped his affable mask, the lines of disappointment and cynicism etched into his face were clear. "A man like me doesn't have friends.

Only sycophants wanting to either pull me down or use me as a stepping stool for their own careers."

"Then you've been in politics too long." Winter's narrow face was pale and stony. "Perhaps it's better for you to get out before it destroys you."

Atwater lifted his shoulders. "I say the same every election. Yet here I am." He spread his hands.

"Let this be the last time, then. In four years, we'll go on a hunting trip to Elkshire. What do you say?"

Atwater laughed again, more sad than bitter this time. "Aye," he agreed and rose to his feet. "I'm telling you the truth, August," he went on earnestly. "I had no idea what the pawnbroker did alongside his lawful business. I saw no ghouls, no demons, no elementals in amongst all the rest of his rubbish."

Winter inclined his head.

"Am I free to go?" Atwater made a questioning gesture.

"I have no further questions," said Winter. "I only ask that you make yourself available if there are other developments."

"I will," promised Atwater. "In exchange, can I trust you'll keep my private affairs to yourself?" He half-turned, including the silent Trey.

"Of course." Winter's voice was weary. Trey gave a sharp, downward jerk of his chin.

Right now, Arabella was his chief concern.

They waited in silence as Atwater left the room. They heard his footsteps, the scuffle of boots as Sutton and Morgan got to their feet, the mutter of voices, the distant slam of the outer door.

Trey turned to Winter.

"Before you say anything," said Winter, "the truth spell did not react during this conversation." He lifted his hand and showed Trey a lattice of silver runes, more complex than anything Trey could create.

"I see." Surprise rippled through Trey. He hadn't expected Winter to do much beyond taking Atwater at his word.

"Of course," Winter mused, staring at the door, "truth spells are known to be notoriously unreliable. But they are not entirely useless. For instance, a well-done truth spell will flicker and change as its subject talks, depending on the rise and fall of his emotions. Did you know that?"

"I confess I haven't studied truth spells in depth, sir. What did yours tell you?"

"My spell did not change at all. Not when Atwater spoke of his embarrassment, not when he showed the weary bitterness behind his mask. He was more honest with me in the last hour than he has in months, and the *truth spell did not change.*"

Trey straightened. "What does that mean?

Winter transferred his gaze from the door to Trey's face. "It means," he said with black humor, "that either I don't deserve the title of Runemaster or that someone put a spell on Atwater to foil any attempts to get intelligence from him."

"You sensed this?" Trey frowned.

"No, but spells that affect the mind can be buried so deep, it would need an entire circle of magicians to ferret them out. Atwater knows more than he's telling, but I cannot force it out of him with the tools currently at my disposal."

"I had not guessed that you were so suspicious, sir." A newfound respect for the man stirred inside Trey. So Winter was more than the usual hidebound aristocrat convinced that there were boundaries no one of his class would dare violate.

"I wasn't chosen to head this Bureau solely on my good looks, Shield."

"Right now, Miss Trent is our only source," pressed Trey. "I'm certain she remembered something important. The Duchess sensed there's something bigger going on and Arabella spoke of miasma. We can't overlook that."

"Miasma is troubling." Winter sat down and pulled a sheet of paper towards him.

Troubling was an understatement.

Miasma was noxious stuff from the Shadow Lands. It could corrode iron, smother elementals, burn flesh. It could reach inside of you, twist your memories, give you nightmares, poison your very soul.

During the Great Incursion, the vanguard of the Demon Lord Astrofael had been armed with weapons of miasma. They had used them to invade the dreams of thousands of people and turn hundreds to their own ends.

Now there were even fewer phantasmists to deal with another incursion from the Shadow Lands. And if they had smuggled miasma into Vaeland…

"I'm going after Arabella," said Trey abruptly. "She's the only one who knows."

"Agreed," said Winter, sketching with a pencil. "It's unfortunate that you hid the girl's presence, but we can discuss that later."

"What?" Trey had expected more resistance.

"You're going into the Shadow Lands to track her." Winter put down his pencil, turned the paper around, and slid it across his desk. Trey leaned over the sketched spell. "But with proper precautions."

Trey perused the page. "It'll be easier if I *don't* leave my body behind."

"And more dangerous. We need to be able to bring you back if things go wrong. Trey," said Winter as he opened his mouth to argue, using his given name for the first time, "you're the only Border Walker we have. Even if miasma is involved—and we don't know for certain that it is, despite what Miss Trent said—I'm not taking undue risks. Understood?"

Winter was not going to budge, Trey saw. He gave a curt nod. "Understood, sir."

Arabella remembered.

She remembered hurrying across the street in the deepening twilight, stumbling in her haste. She remembered thinking how quickly the gloom had fallen over the Fleet, huddled in the shadow of All Saints'.

She remembered being uncertain, afraid, half-wishing she had never set out on this mad scheme to save Harry from the clutches of his creditors—or worse, a scolding from his father.

She knew, none better, how a guardian's displeasure could hurt.

Arabella clung to the door handle of the pawnshop as if it were a life line. She barely noticed the stuffed crocodile head in the grimy window as she eased open the door. Its single bell shivered but didn't ring out, so timid and quiet was her entrance.

Arabella edged into the shop, eyes wide. A deeper gloom shrouded the place, this one old and musty and comprised of shadows accumulated over the years. It was a treasure cave and a pirate's hoard all at once—that is, if kings and pirates collected boxes of shoes, sticks of furniture, cross china cats, and tarnished trinkets.

There was no one behind the counter, but voices emanated from a back room. Arabella called out, "Hello?", but her mouth was so dry, her attitude so hesitant, it didn't come out above a breath.

The murmured conversation came to her in ebbs and flows, in sentence fragments and half-heard words. One voice was nasal and high-pitched, with a whine in it that ran like fingernails down Arabella's nerves. The other…

The other she couldn't recall at all.

But the nasal voice went on and on, seeming to rise in agitation. Arabella heard, "… miasma… dangerous… compressed into globes… at the Viewing…"

The other voice soothed. At least, that's what Arabella thought even though she could neither remember its sound or the words it spoke. The nasal voice lowered as if placated.

Arabella shifted in discomfort, not liking being an inadvertent eavesdropper, not liking the tenor of the conversation. Lord Atwater or no, she wanted to be out of here. She backed towards the door.

Just as the curtain partitioning the back room from the shop rippled, as if being drawn back.

Arabella seized the handle, opened the door, and then shut it with a slam. The bell jangled as the curtain was whipped aside.

She stood there, looking around, as if she'd just come in.

The man who'd drawn the curtain back was thin and stooped, with stringy hair and narrow eyes. Alarm, surprise, and displeasure flickered across his face in quick succession, then vanished. An oily smile stretched his lips and a hard, speculative gleam came into his eyes.

Arabella disliked him at once, but she fixed a smile on her face and hoped it didn't look too forced.

"Well, well, young lady," said the man. He clasped his hands together in what he probably thought was a genial manner. "What can I help you with?"

This was the owner of the nasal whine. Arabella went forward, though it was a wrench to leave her station by the exit and walk further into the pawnbroker's lair. "Are you Mr. Gibbs?" she asked, referencing the name on the sign and cocking her head in a manner she knew was charming. "I have a small financial *problem* I hope you can assist me with?"

Another person stepped out from behind Gibbs. Arabella said, in feigned surprise, "Oh, are you busy?" She retreated a step, closer to the door again.

"No, no," said Gibbs. "My visitor was just leaving."

The visitor was—and here Arabella experienced another mystifying blank in her memory. She couldn't recollect anything about this person. Man or woman, young or old, thin or plump, dark-haired or blonde or bald or grey: nothing. The person moved across the room, heading for the door. Arabella edged out of the way, or tried to. Somehow, in the maze of narrow paths that wound through tottering piles, she bumped into the other instead.

"I'm so sorry!" Her own exclamation rang in her ears. "I beg your pardon!"

Another blank.

"Oh, but I have people waiting for me outside." The lie was so patently false, Arabella was sure it was written all over her face.

Another moment of nothingness, of words forgotten from a face now removed from her memory.

"Thank you for your concern," she said again, holding out her hand. She received *something* from the mysterious person; she remembered the feel of it brushing across her fingers. There was a confusing tangle of bright lights and a feeling of dizziness, of the room distorting out of focus, wavering, then snapping back into detail and color.

Arabella was in a pawnshop, the owner smirking at her from behind the counter, saying something obsequious that she couldn't quite make out until her ears popped.

There were only the two of them in the shop. There always had been from the moment she entered, the door handle slipping out of her grasp with a bang, the bell clanging in a tinny cacophony.

Arabella came to herself in a place so dark, it seemed like light had never touched it. She felt nothing around her, not solid ground under her feet nor a breath of air nor a shake of sound. Nothing to tell her if she was in a cellar or a music room or underwater or anything.

She could've been suspended over the maw of a kraken and never known it.

Arabella's breath hitched. Her limbs thrashed, involuntarily, her aethereal body trying to find a way out of this darkness.

Bands snapped around her, searing her substance. Arabella may have screamed, but she couldn't hear it above the sizzle and buzz of the runes. She was clenched into a ball of pain and she... couldn't... breathe.

She struggled and the bands tightened even more. It wasn't just the pain, it was the feeling of being held down, straitjacketed, bound. The feeling of being helpless while waiting for others to *do* things to you. Of not being able to run or fight or resist.

Stay calm! she told herself. *Panicking only makes things worse.*

She forced herself to hold still. Forced herself to take deep breaths, even though she was a ghost and didn't need to. Forced herself to clear her mind. Forced herself to be as uncaring as air, as malleable as water, as solid as the earth.

The old tricks still worked. The fluttering feeling inside her, that of a wild bird beating against the bars of its cage, subsided. One by one, the bands loosened and slipped off. The agony of their searing became an ache, then a memory.

Cautiously, Arabella extended senses she had never wanted to use again. There was magic around her, and if she wanted to get out, she needed to use what little power, what meager experience she had.

She hung in a cylinder narrower than her arm span. The pentagram was small, much smaller than the one Trey had used. At least he'd given her space to walk in, and light, and his wards hadn't hurt as much. Almost she missed it.

This pentagram, however, did not bode well for the intentions of the person who'd yanked her out of Merrimack's and trapped her here.

She had no idea how much time had passed since she'd felt those painful hooks dragging her away from Trey. She remembered him springing for her, remembered telling him what she had dredged from her memory.

Her fingertips tingled where their hands had touched.

He was a Border Walker, a phantasmist, the Shade Hunter. He'd be able to track her. Wouldn't he?

She just needed to be patient and not give in to panic.

And then she heard it.

A sound brushed the edge of her hearing, half-rasp, half-moan. Prickles ran all over Arabella.

There was *something* prowling outside the pentagram. And it wasn't at all friendly. A smell came to her—the chill of ice, the tang of blood, and the sweetish reek of death. The combination made her sick; she'd have retched if she weren't a ghost who'd had nothing to eat in days.

Whatever was out there touched the wards. They hissed in a fountain of painful sparks. Arabella hugged herself, trying to make herself smaller, afraid to set them off again.

A voice, like the scrape of manacles against each other, said, "What a pretty morsel we caught. An uncorrupted spirit, fluttering, fluttering. Come here, pretty butterfly."

It dripped hunger and promised pain. Arabella shivered and pressed her lips together.

"I hear you," the voice continued. "I hear the pulse of your fear, like the racing heartbeat of a bird. A pretty little bird with bright eyes, whose neck I can snap with one hand."

It laughed now, the noise like that of a stone lid dragging across a sarcophagus.

Arabella said, keeping her voice even, "Are you the ghoul that killed Mr. Gibbs?"

"Pshaw." It made a wet, disgusted sound. "Such a small, shriveled, sooty soul that was. I am hungry for a better meal."

Its yearning came at her in waves even through the barrier, raking across her being like claws of poison. Arabella felt nauseated, but she told herself that since she had no stomach, it didn't matter.

The ghoul was ready to talk and Arabella was happy to let it. In spite of the way its voice scraped down her soul, this was her chance to get intelligence out of it.

"That couldn't have been very pleasant," she said sympathetically. "Why him and not someone more"—she searched for the right word—"tender?"

It hissed, its displeasure acid in Arabella's incorporeal body. She winced. "I do what Master tells me to."

"Oh, I see. Makes sense. We wouldn't want anyone else to find out about the miasma at the Viewing."

It laughed again. This time Arabella was forcefully reminded of bones rattling. "Miasma's only the start of the plan, little butterfly. Master—" It broke off, choking, as if one of the bones had stuck in its throat.

Arabella rather hoped it had.

But that wasn't it. Someone else was in the space—Arabella refused to name it a room without further confirmation—a presence whose words and voice disappeared from her memory within moments.

The presence said, *You talk too much.*

A strangled sound answered him. Arabella almost heard the ghoul's words die, stillborn, before they could be said.

The other turned its attention to Arabella. Already, its voice had faded from her memory.

It had to be the one from the pawnshop. *Master*, the ghoul had called him.

You've been a naughty girl, Miss Trent, poking your nose in business not your own.

"It's more accurate to say I was dragged into this business," said Arabella with spirit. "What do you mean by trapping me here?"

I was curious and wished the pleasure of your company.

"You could've called upon me, instead of resorting to such tactics, if that were truly your intention." Arabella tried to focus on the other's words, to hold them in her memory, but it was like cupping water. Sooner or later, the water trickled through her fingers and she was left with an odd, one-sided conversation, blanks where the Master's words ought to be. "But I suppose detaining a lady's spirit is of a little concern to those smuggling miasma into the mortal plane."

Ah, so you pulled that out from your memory, did you? I was right to consider you a threat.

Arabella, straining to hold on to the other's voice, caught a wet chewing sound, a whiff of something both sweet and sour.

"Whatever you're planning won't work, you know. The Phantasm Bureau will apprehend you. There's no doubt about it." Her words were brave, but her heart doubted. What had Trey said about the Great Incursion? It had decimated the Bureau's ranks.

Let them try. The presence scoffed at the idea. *What can they do without Trey Shield?*

Warning bells rang in her mind. "What do you mean?" The question came out short and sharp.

Had she revealed too much? Arabella bit her ghostly lip, the sensation like walking into a fog.

He's coming for you.

"Perhaps," she said cautiously. No need to let the ghoul's master uncover her hope.

I'm depending on it.

The Master laughed, a sinister sound that sent fear thrilling through her. And then the presence left, taking the ghoul with it.

She forgot its last words moments after it left. But the sense of them lingered, like a nightmare, along with that tang in the air she couldn't place.

It was expecting Trey. Planned for it, in fact.

This was a trap, and she was the bait.

Chapter Twelve

IT WAS HARD TO HANG in the dark, feeling helpless. Arabella's entire body was tight with the need to do *something*.

She didn't want to lead Trevelyan Shield into a trap. And she rather doubted the Master would let her go afterwards. She shuddered, remembering the ghoul's hunger.

I'd prefer to take my chances in the Shadow Lands than with that creature!

She started at the thought.

The Shadow Lands. All evening, the realm had been near to her, peeking over her shoulder, breathing down her neck, drawing her closer. If she could go into the Shadow Lands, she had a chance of finding Trey and warning him before he was captured.

Arabella turned her thoughts towards the place, remembering its haunting music, smoke-thick walls, and frozen souls. It was nearby, but just out of her reach.

The wards were in the way.

She'd have to do something about them first. But what? It was pitch-dark; she couldn't make out the construction of the pentagram.

It was silly. Here she was—a spirit who didn't need food or water or sleep, who could slide through walls and doors as easily as if slipping through water.

And she needed light?

What if I made my own light?

There were spirits who glowed. Why couldn't she?

Arabella held her hands in front of her face—or where she thought her face was.

Shine, she told them and let the memories flow.

Silver moonlight flooding through a window… a cat's eyes reflecting amber in the night… greyish wisps fluttering over dark moors… fungi glowing a sickly-green under a tree where a suicide had hung… blue luminescence on the dark seas coming in with the tide…

… the blank eyes of a corpse kindling to unholy life… the snap and crackle of a demonic fire…

Arabella's throat tightened; something beat against her non-existent ribcage. She forced herself to move on from the images, to gas lamps burning yellow on Lumen's streets, to runes gleaming silver, to dancing under a star-washed sky with a man's hand clasping hers and his arm around her waist.

Heat that had nothing to do with light or flame rushed through Arabella.

She gasped.

In front of her were her own hands, fingers small and delicate, softly glowing. Arabella glanced down and saw that her entire form was illuminated, hints of shining color shifting throughout it.

I did it, she thought, triumphant, but tired. She was drained and felt more insubstantial than ever, as if burning away her essence sliver by sliver.

Even as she watched, she grew even more tissue-thin.

Hurry! What's the use of this, if you're just going to burn up without doing anything?

Arabella looked at the wards and grimaced.

They weren't made of runes, the way Trey's were. These were twisted spikes of life energy, unhappy and cruel, growing in thorns and rusty tangles of wire.

No wonder they had attacked her so viciously.

But this was magic she was familiar with.

Through the wards, Arabella faintly made out a cavernous space, emptiness stretching away into darkness. A warehouse, she guessed. She stretched out her senses, hoping to catch a whiff of mud and water. Nothing.

But underneath her...

Arabella floated midway up a cylinder. The pentagram was on the floor beneath her, a construct of bone and hair and rope from a hangman's noose. Caught in the knotted middle of it gleamed something round and small and blue.

Her sapphire ring.

So that's how they found me and brought me here!

Arabella reached down for it, pushing through air that was surprisingly dense. It resisted, pushing back. Arabella lost her balance, spun, brushed close to the wards.

They hissed and spat, cat-like.

Arabella kept her arms tight by her side. For several moments, she didn't move at all, though she felt the light consuming her substance.

Could a soul really go up in a flare like this? She wished she'd paid better attention in church. Her theological education was woefully meager.

Right. One more try at this, I think. Arabella lifted her right hand and concentrated her substance into it. It solidified, but her clothes had frayed to wisps and the ends of her hair to mist.

Arabella dove.

She swam like a fish in water, arms to her side, kicking with her legs. Her initial rush got her close to the tangle, reaching out with her more solid hand, before the spell began to push her away.

She gritted her teeth, eyes fixed on that ring.

Please, God-Father and Risen Lord! I need that! She stretched, her arm extending impossibly long. She felt ghostly bones detach and ghostly muscles elongate. Her shoulder softened, her elbow disappeared.

And still her fingers, glowing strongly, reached.

Reached through the pentagram's tangle. Brushed past spines and bristles and thorns that scratched and pierced but could not stop. Grasped the ring, cold and hard and shiny.

Yes! I'm glad I practiced being a pokey. Arabella reeled in her substance, like a fisherman with a line.

The ring lifted out of the spell.

And the spell went insane.

The curved bones and sharp spines shuddered. Rope and hair whipped. The walls of the cylinder sizzled.

The air around Arabella boiled and buffeted, burned and stung. She would've screamed, if it hadn't felt like her mouth was scalded, her eyes scorched away.

All she could feel was the ring in her fingers and the Shadow Lands, cool at her back.

She didn't even pause to think. As the spell collapsed around her in screeching fury, Arabella turned and plunged into the Shadow Lands.

Arabella landed with a thump, the impact reverberating all through her substance. The solidity was so unexpected, she gasped.

It was as if she had *bones* again. And flesh and—Arabella unclenched her hand.

Her mother's ring was small and solid on her palm. Still shaking from her ordeal, Arabella slid it onto her finger. It settled in place, the star in the heart of the sapphire winking. It was a friendly glimmer, and for a moment her mother's scent of kitchen herbs and stillroom potions surrounded Arabella, giving her courage.

Thank you, Mama.

Arabella didn't wonder long about how she'd brought the material ring into the Shadow Lands, nor how it was able to fit onto her spirit hand. Trey, she was sure, had a prosy book somewhere with several possible explanations. In the meantime, she'd accept this as a gift from the God-Father, and vow to never let herself be so foolishly parted from her mother's memento again.

Arabella scrambled to her feet, looked around, and stared.

She had expected an entirely different place from this, a place thick with gloom or fog, seething with demons and the unquiet dead. She had braced herself to run—or fight.

Instead, Arabella found herself by the side of a quiet lake. The light was pale gold, thin and without warmth, emanating from a sky the color of old honey. She could make out no sun. The ground underfoot was covered in dry brown grass, frosted over. It crunched under her feet, and cold seeped through the soles of her kid slippers.

She was back in her spotted morning dress, a rather incongruous choice for her current location.

Stunted trees with bone-white limbs, like skeletons of themselves, dotted the landscape. Strings of beads, ropes of shells, slips of paper, and more hung from the leafless branches. They tinkled and clicked, sighed and murmured, in a small breath of wind. Arabella caught words in the stirring air and decided not to walk among the trees. She didn't want to be caught and tangled in the thoughts of others like she had at Merrimack's.

She thought it would be rather worse here.

Instead, Arabella turned towards the lake. It glimmered grey and silver, with odd, heaving ropes of color here and there.

A man stood on the bank, dressed in baggy trousers, shapeless coat, and rumpled cap. He was fishing, his back towards her.

The entire scene went suddenly very still. Arabella stood poised, unsure whether to flee.

A distant cry, mournful and moving, broke the silence. Arabella glanced up at the sky as a bird arrowed across it, dark against the dulled bronze.

It might be a duck, except it was angled instead of curved, as if made out of knife-cuts.

The fisherman paid neither her nor the bird any heed. Beyond him, in the distance, was an edifice, the color of burnt caramel. It was sticky-looking, as if it had been molded rather than built.

Something tugged her in that direction. She didn't know if she would find her body or Trey there, but either possibility was preferable to staying here. She had no idea how time flowed in the Shadow Lands, how much of the night in Vaeland had already past.

Her exorcism was set for Saturday morning. She had to be back in her body before them.

Arabella hurried towards the structure, her footprints dark in the grass. She hesitated as she passed the fisherman, then shook her head. Why borrow trouble in these strange realms? Her experiences with the dead hadn't been pleasant so far.

She made to go on, lifting a foot.

The man said, without turning, "Did you leave behind a true love, miss?"

A thrill ran through Arabella. For a wild moment, Trey Shield's face flashed through her mind. Ruthlessly she quashed the thought. She was no romantic ninny to fall in love with her rescuer.

"No," she said firmly, both to herself and the fisherman.

"Pity," he answered. Muscles bunched under his jacket as he jerked his line out of the water. Something narrow and silver thrashed at the end of it.

Intrigued, Arabella drifted closer, wondering what manner of fish existed in the Shadow Lands.

The fisherman reached out and held the line several inches above the writhing creature. The fish had silver scales tinged with rainbow colors, but what drew Arabella's attention was the membranous frill at its tail and fins and around its neck.

That, and its eyes, round specks of startling blue, as if it bore chips of turquoise in its head.

"What sort of fish is it?" she whispered to the fisherman. In profile he looked quite normal, a sturdy man with weathered skin and ruddy cheeks and the shadow of a beard on his cheeks and chin. His hair curled black under the felt cap and his dark eyebrows were thick and straight.

"Lover's Last Words," said the man. Gently, he detached a silver hook from the gasping fish's mouth and tenderly, he held the creature in one hand. The fish wriggled weakly as the man lowered his lips to kiss it.

And then he tilted his head up, opened his mouth, dropped the fish in, and swallowed it whole.

Arabella skipped back in alarm. She could *see* his neck ripple, oddly loose, as the fish slithered down it. The front of his yellowed shirt billowed, then settled.

The fisherman licked his lips with a tongue much too long and pink, like a cat's. He grimaced. "She told her lover she loved him, but her affections were tempered with resentment. Resentment that she was dying while he still lived, resentment because she knew that he was young and would someday find another to love. It leaves a bitter aftertaste.

"It always does."

Once again he cast his line, the silver hook, unbaited, flying through the air.

"Are you sure," he said again, craning to look at Arabella, "you have no lover?"

"Very much so," said Arabella, her mind thoroughly made up by the fisherman's strange actions.

His dark eyes were curiously blank, the irises swallowed up by the pupils. His mouth was twisted with regret. Words unspoken and words unheard seemed to linger around him. Arabella felt them, a scrape of bitterness, like vinegar splashed across her soul.

"Someday," said the fisherman with ageless patience, "someday, I'll taste words that are sweet and joyous, like honey." And with that he turned his face away and took notice of her no more.

Arabella tip-toed away from the lake and the odd man, rustling through dried grasses. Frost-limned bracken snapped underfoot. Withered flowers of silver and lavender, still clinging to the heather, crumbled as she brushed past them.

Pools of water, like shards of a broken mirror, gleamed here and there in the grass. Arabella stayed away from them, afraid of what she might see.

A path appeared in front of her, packed hard and brown, skimmed with a milky layer of ice. Arabella stepped on it gingerly, but it felt waxy rather than slippery. She quickened her pace towards the building she had seen from the grove of skeletal trees.

Up closer, the structure reminded Arabella of a sadly lopsided layered cake. It had a softened look, the architectural features—balconies, casements, turrets, molding—all running together. The castle, or so she thought it had once been, hadn't crumbled so much as melted.

Yellow lights flickered in shapeless windows. Arabella climbed up the steps, brown and sticky; through a portico that smelled like yesterday's baking; and into the open doorway.

She crossed a short stretch of what she hoped was only red carpet and stood at the top of a grand stairway, looking down into an immense ballroom filled with people. The chamber stood open to a cloudy night sky, moon and stars veiled from sight. Men and women, dressed in costumes of all kinds, from straight white robes to hooped skirts to knee-length tunics and sandals crisscrossing over bare legs, swirled around. Their chatter and laughter filled the space with a kind of tiny roar, like the sound of the ocean in a sea shell.

Arabella descended the stairs, each step rounded and hard like fossilized bread. It was covered in velvety green carpeting that on closer inspection resembled furry mold. The balustrade was riddled with holes, and Arabella could've sworn she saw something wriggle in one of them. She lifted her skirt and walked carefully, trying not to touch anything.

The floor of the chamber, when she got to it, was spongy, with many dimples and rises. Groups of partygoers stood gossiping and eating around small tables draped in cobweb and piled with bruised fruit, rancid meat, and stale bread. The guests themselves wore tattered clothes, and their substance was worn so thin, Arabella could only see some of them if she squinted.

They ignored her as she passed, each one holding a separate conversation.

"And so I told Gehenna-bai…"

"The rains are late this year…"

"I do so love a tea made from broken hearts steeped in the tears of the disinherited!"

"Has the messenger come? Tell me, has the messenger come?"

The last was spoken by a ghost so transparent and agitated that he was a mere flutter in the air. Arabella could barely make out a middle-aged man with staring eyes and care-lined face, wearing a loin cloth and a tiger's skin around his shoulders, his body smeared with paint.

For a moment, Arabella's eyes connected with his. A jolt ran through her. Then the ghost faded away entirely, leaving only a small insistent, "… the messenger come?" before it, too, dwindled into a sigh and was gone.

No one else had noticed. They continued their prattle, in voices that were higher, louder, and faster than before.

Shaken, Arabella followed that inner pull to the shadows on the other side of the ballroom. A cavernous gloom shrouded this end, and the few guests nearby stood with their backs turned towards it.

The darkness exhaled a warm breeze that smelled of wet earth and wild grass. Arabella glanced at the chamber behind her, a place safe in the same way a prison was. It was a roadhouse that everyone was petrified to leave.

She didn't want to end up like that barely-there ghost who had winked out right before her eyes.

Resolutely she turned, consulted her intuition, and strode into the darkness.

The sound of dripping water accompanied her long before the darkness lifted. Arabella brushed against wet leaves, tipping water into her slippers. A few moments of concentration, and the slippers became half-boots with sturdy heels. That was better.

The path was soggy and she *squelched*. Every now and then, something thin and woody tickled the back of her neck. Arabella *hoped* it was a twig and not a skeletal hand.

The thought made her quicken her pace through the undergrowth. Arabella tripped over a root and caught herself from falling. Her hands clutched something muscular and vine-like. It writhed and Arabella hastily let go.

Her unseen surroundings closed in, snagging painfully in her hair, reaching out across the path. Branches whipped in her face, and she splashed muddy water over herself with every step.

It was cold and disgusting.

So intent was she upon her footing, Arabella didn't notice the creature until much later.

Something moved in the foliage, much quieter, keeping pace with her. She heard its breathing, low and soft.

The back of her neck prickled. Arabella stood still, peering, but could make out nothing.

It kept its distance.

Arabella couldn't just stand there in the dark, waiting for it to make a move. She pressed on, uncomfortably aware of her unseen companion.

The darkness lightened, turning to a thick smoky grey. Shapes appeared out of it—a tree trunk, a tangle of large leaves, some hanging vines. White fog moved sluggishly as she passed through it, leaving warm moisture on her face.

Arabella's legs ached, as if she'd been trudging through a marsh for days. Tiredness bowed her shoulders. Heat and humidity pressed down on her.

She wondered if ghosts perspired. It was hard to tell, with the damp plastering her hair to her head and sticking her clothes to her body. Her shoes and hem were waterlogged.

In this realm, it seemed she retained all the inconveniences of her corporeal form.

The light was a pearly grey when Arabella stopped by a quiet brook and leaned against a tree. It was cooler under the canopy, and the gurgle of water as it slipped over a bed of dark stones a welcome change from the ceaseless dripping.

She stared idly at the stones, noting the way they glinted with veins of green and blue. They reminded Arabella of lapis lazuli imported from the Goblin Empire. She leaned down for a closer look.

A snarl ripped the silence. A sinuous, feline body leapt out of the trees. It landed on the bank and turned in one savage fluid movement. Flash of fangs, ripple of spotted pelt, green glare of lantern eyes.

Arabella yelped and ran.

Her feet took flight. She skimmed over the brook, over the roots of ancient trees, over a tangle of undergrowth. The large cat bounded behind her, its rumble never far from her ears. Its breath was hot against her shoulder blades.

Branches whipped by. She dodged around trunks, scraped her arms against roughened bark. The exertion burned through her and roared in her ears, punctuated by her own scared whimpers.

She didn't have time to think, just flee, following the pull inside her. Her body in Vaeland, still drawing her like a magnet, from so far away.

There. A gap in the trees, a golden arch framing light. Arabella tumbled into a clearing filled with sparkling sunshine, and fell to her knees.

The sweet green scent of crushed grass rose to her nose.

This was followed by a gentle laugh.

"Welcome," said a voice, full of mirth and warmth. "Welcome, weary traveler."

Arabella squinted in the direction of the voice as her eyes adjusted to the light. A woman resolved out of the golden smear, tall, black-haired, pale-skinned. Faint lines around her eyes and mouth put her at about middle age.

She wore an old-fashioned fitted gown of red velvet, a golden girdle low about her slender waist, emphasizing the curves of her hips. The skirts were full to her feet, her sleeves tight on her arms, and her shoulders bare above the low boat-shaped neckline.

"Who are you?" Arabella blurted out, too tired and too scared for proper etiquette.

The woman chuckled. "My, you are a blunt one. Spirited, too." She surveyed Arabella with kindly satisfaction. "But those are the only ones who make it this far." Sadness touched her voice and the brightness in her face dimmed.

As if on cue, the large cat set up an eerie scream. Arabella sensed its frustrated energy outside the clearing as it prowled.

She scrambled to her feet, still tensed to run. "You didn't answer my question," she told the woman. Kindly or not, ordinary-seeming or not, she was still a denizen of the Shadow Lands.

The woman bowed her dark head, a slender gold coronet gleaming against her hair. "Forgive me. I am Shahandra, one of the Guardians of this place. It is my task to provide a small refuge for those unfortunate enough to lose themselves in the Shadow Lands, to give them a reprieve from its dangers."

She gestured around her. Arabella noted a number of grey tree-stumps, each polished to a shine, functioning as tables. Each held a profusion of objects—a tangle of jewelry on one, a host of goblets on another, stacks of plates, rows of daggers, folded clothing, and more.

Arabella's fingers itched to snatch up a weapon. She put her hands behind her back lest her desires get the better of her. "Where did you get all these?"

Shahandra did not seem to mind her curtness. She answered with a gracious patience that made Arabella feel small and churlish. "I create them from the aether within the Shadow Lands."

Arabella paused, thinking of Trey's sword and the stool he had conjured up. "I thought aether was grey?"

"In the mortal realm, it is," said Shahandra. "Here in the Shadow Lands, I have more… flexibility."

"How long have you been here?" asked Arabella, but the woman was already turning away to a slender, moon-pale pedestal. She dipped a silver chalice into a stone bowl atop it and came forward with a friendly smile.

"Drink," Shahandra said, holding it out. The cuffs of her sleeves extended up to her fingers. "You must be thirsty. The Shadow Lands sap your strength. Drink, and refresh yourself."

Looking into that clear water, Arabella realized she was indeed desperately parched.

Without thinking, she reached out her hand.

The cat screamed again, the sound clawing down her nerves. Arabella jumped, and the whole clearing wavered in her sight. She frowned and rubbed her eyes, but the smear refused to clear. It was as if she were seeing double, one image on top of the other.

Arabella looked at Shahandara, who smiled with mild concern, still whole and solid, holding out the chalice. "I fear that you are rapidly losing substance," she went on. "Drink and be restored."

Thirst burned in Arabella's throat. Her insides felt withered. She yearned for that water with a ferocity that shocked her.

Her hands clenched into fists. Pain shot through her right finger—her mother's ring biting deep into her incorporeal flesh, insistent.

Arabella looked down at it. The sapphire glowed.

A slight frown marred Shahandra's smooth white forehead. "You come bearing some interesting magic," she said. Her voice came from far away. The rippling of the clearing around her made Arabella sick to her stomach. It was as if something was straining to come out of the very fabric of the place itself, like children revealing themselves from behind draperies.

Her hand throbbed, the ring a band of heat around her finger.

"Ah, you're in pain," said Shahandra. "Quickly, take it off and cast it aside before it consumes you!"

Did the Master cast black magic on Mama's ring? Arabella wrenched it off her finger. Sparks shot up her arms. She raised her hand to fling it away.

And remembered.

She remembered this pain.

It was the same as the time she went through the barrier at All Saints'. A fierce, purifying sort of pain.

The ache was concentrated in her eyes. Her vision was washed with white. Arabella had the sense that someone was trying to tell her something. Something important.

"Hurry!" Shahandra said urgently.

On impulse, Arabella held the ring up to her right eye, peeping through the hole.

She stifled a squeak.

The warm golden light that had suffused the clearing was gone, replaced with a cold silver one. Twisted and blackened tree stumps tore through the soggy ground like rotten teeth. Each bore a clutter of relics in rusted and tottering piles—wicked knives with serrated edges, blood-stained clothing, cracked goblets, and chipped plates.

Shahandra too had changed, her skin a dead white, leached of all life. Her ebony tresses twined and hissed like snakes, her coronet was a rusted circle of iron thorns. The woman's eyes were chips of obsidian and her dress stained with things Arabella did not wish to identify.

In her hands was a human skull, full of a thick and dark liquid.

"Drink," she said, reaching out, speaking in a voice that seemed to emanate from the grave itself. "Drink!"

"Absolutely not!" Arabella slapped the skull out of Shahandra's hands. It clattered to the ground, spilling foul ooze.

Shahandra gnashed her teeth. Her jaw came unhinged, scales crept up her face.

She lunged at Arabella.

Arabella skipped back and yelled, "Cat! Come!"

It worked. With a snarl and a pounce, the cat was there, in the clearing. Arabella ducked behind Shahandra, now writhing, her dress clinging to her lengthening body.

The cat hit the woman in the chest. They both went down in a whirl of fur and scale, hissing and spitting.

Arabella fled to the other side of the clearing, slipping the ring back on her finger. She glanced at the weapons as she passed, each one full of malice and pain and bloodlust.

She didn't want any of them. She ran.

Moments—or hours—later, Arabella came out of the forest and into a narrow valley, filled with stones and pebbles.

Here she paused. Because instead of *one* pull, she felt two.

They led in different directions.

And for the first time she could see them, manifested as two slender threads, faintly gleaming.

She had no idea which one to follow.

A woman's voice, pleasant and well-bred, said, "One leads back to your body, the other to the one who came into the Shadow Lands."

Arabella spun to face the woman seated on a boulder.

Not another one!

Arabella eyed her warily, this woman with pale hair slipping out of its knot, in a dress with fuller skirts and lower waist than current trends indicated. She sat as if she had all the time in the world.

At Arabella's expression, the woman shrugged and said, "See for yourself."

Arabella bent down and touched one thread. A familiar sensation ran through her—she smelled Aunt Cecilia's perfume, the powder she dusted her neck and arms with, and clean sheets warm from the sun.

The other thread felt as if spun of steel, hard and biting, leading somewhere wilder, colder.

She looked at the woman again and thought she looked familiar. "I'm sorry, but have we met?"

"No, never," said the other composedly. Her hands were clasped loosely in her lap; there was something very restful about her.

Arabella frowned, unable to shake off the nagging feeling she'd seen the woman before. It was hard to tell the color of her eyes save that they were light, and the moonlit glow had bleached her hair to silver.

"I beg your pardon, ma'am," said Arabella gravely, "but I must perform a test."

The woman inclined her head in assent. Arabella pulled off her mother's ring and, feeling foolish but determined, peered at her through it.

The woman remained the same, as did her surroundings.

"You ran across Shahandra," she guessed as Arabella replaced the ring.

"I did." Arabella made a face.

"It took me," said the woman, expressionless, "two years to disentangle myself from the sorceress's clutches."

"I had help," said Arabella, thinking of the cat. "Was she really a Guardian?"

"Once. But it's not good for anyone to linger in the Shadow Lands. Not even the purest can resist the taint."

Arabella gave her a speaking look.

The woman smiled. "Oh, I haven't been here that long. Only about nine years by mortal reckoning. I will move on soon—whether or not I accomplish my purpose."

"And what is that, ma'am?" queried Arabella.

"Right now, it's to tell you what your choices are," answered the woman dryly. "Have you picked?"

Arabella gave a longing look at the thread that led back to her body, to safety and home and warmth.

"This one." Arabella picked the thread of steel, winding it between her fingers. It stung, but not as much as she'd expected.

She had to do it. She had to take the chance that the one looking for her in the Shadow Lands was Trey, not the ghoul nor its Master. If she didn't find Trey, he could still be drawn into the trap.

And there wasn't much time left in which to warn him of the coming attack on the Mirror of Elsinore.

The woman nodded. "Very well, then. Off you go. You haven't a lot of time." There was nothing in her straightforward tone to tell Arabella whether she'd chosen rightly or not.

Arabella started up the path—of course it had to wind uphill into broken, stony country. Then she paused and turned around. "Thank you, ma'am. And," she added impulsively, "I hope it goes well with you, in the end."

A smile flickered on the woman's face. "And you, too, Arabella Trent."

Arabella started but the woman was gone.

She was alone, holding the shining thread. It jerked in her hands. "I'm coming," she told it and resumed climbing.

Halfway up the path, a howl rose up behind her. It echoed against the flat sky above, filled her ears with thunder.

Arabella peered over her shoulder as the dark bulk of a monster heaved itself up over the landscape. *Oh no!*

Run!

Chapter Thirteen

TREY ARRIVED FIRST, AS HE always did when walking the Shadow Lands in spirit, at the place he called Wildcross.

This was the Shadow Lands version of Whitecross Abbey, the ancestral home of the Shields. But here, the bow-shaped lake was darker and deeper, the drop from hilltop to lake a straight plunge, as if cut by a knife. No house overlooked the lake, though the Shadow Lands kept trying to manifest one.

The trouble with houses was that they tended to attract inhabitants.

An old ash tree stood in the place occupied by Whitecross Abbey in the mortal plane. Its bark was a pale grey, its branches spread silvery-green leaflets up to a tarnished sky. Clouds of aether, fine and white, stretched like cobwebs overhead.

Trey put a hand on the ridged, diamond-textured bark, felt the flow of pure sap in the heart of the tree. The ash protected this corner of the Shadow Lands, and every summer and winter he renewed the rites that kept it pure and strong. Its unseen roots plunged through the soft, unstable ground and anchored in Vaelish soil.

This was an outpost, a small, safe place in a hostile land.

The ground around the ash was fuzzy with the short blades that passed for Shadow Lands grass. They rubbed against his spirit like razor burn. The land rolled around him in sullen hillocks and dispirited hollows. Intermittent items of interest broke the monotony—a stand of sickly-pale birches; a topiary shaped like a knight on a charger, clipped to within an inch of its life; a well in a hollow.

Most of these were temporary; save for the well, they changed as the seasons passed. Trey guessed, like the roots of the ash, the well too drew its water from good Vaelish soil. He had never figured out where on the actual estate it was, however. This made him leery of taking a sip, despite the winch and wooden bucket hanging above it.

Once assured that this place was as safe as the Shadow Lands could ever be, Trey stepped away, questing for Arabella.

Time and space were fluid in this realm. It might've taken one moment to snatch Arabella from Merrimack's courtyard and spirit her to her present location, but from his perspective, her route could be long, tedious, and meandering.

And most probably, dangerous.

Trey pulled a wry face as he looked down at the cuff on his wrist. A band of silver with darker threads running through it, it connected him to his body in Vaeland—and to Sutton's overseeing, Winter's runes, and other magic besides.

He felt like small child on leading strings.

But these were the conditions Winter had set, so Trey dismissed the feeling and drew phantasmia from around him.

Phantasmia was the potent magic of the Shadow Lands, far more dangerous than aether, not as malevolent as miasma. Trey's use of it in Vaeland was severely curtailed, but here, he could give full rein to his gift.

Here, he could really *be* a phantasmist.

The strange, half-alive stuff of the Shadow Lands coalesced inside his hands like thick smoke. Trey spun it into fine wires and sent them looping off in a hundred different directions. He breathed memories of Arabella into them and cast them out to go seek.

Now was the part he hated.

He had to wait.

If he'd brought his body, he could've tracked her himself. Trey surveyed the dull landscape, his gaze arrested by the black smear on the distant horizon.

Memory supplied the features he couldn't distinguish. It was the ruined city, of course, never far from Wildcross, a constant reminder of his oldest failure. Border Walkers before him had searched their whole lives for just a glimpse of the place; meanwhile, he could never quite shake it off.

Even from here, he could taste bitter despair on the air. If he strained, he'd hear the toll of its tongueless bells. He knew, none better, how it'd warp the sky and land around it, turning them into a swamp of miasma.

He had to act, before the city's presence jeopardized the already fraught operation.

Sorry, Winter.

Trey paced away from the ash, down the gentle slope away from the lake and past the well.

Despite what the vista promised, it didn't take long for him to reach the boundary of Wildcross. The mist beyond was colored like ice, with hints of blue and purple. There was a weighty feel to it; Trey could sense it trying to solidify enough to form something. His eyes narrowed.

A trap?

For him—or Arabella?

He crooked his left hand and Sorrow flashed into shape in his fingers. Here, she was even more glorious, like iced lightning, with intricate patterns etched in quicksilver on the blade.

There was a tug on one of his lines, one that led straight into the mist. A strong pull, and with it the scent of rain and sun-warmed linen.

If there was ever a scent of Arabella Trent, this was it.

Wait, Winter had cautioned. *Don't go out to her. Reel her in.*

Sorry, Winter. I can't do that with wraiths about to be born.

He strode across the boundary of his safe place. The cuff around his wrist tightened, followed by a pinch between his shoulders.

Trey reached behind him and detached the line there. It crumbled to a wisp.

It would take Winter and Sutton at least a quarter of an hour to hook him again.

That was enough time for him.

And with that, he swung Sorrow in an arc through the torso of a newly-formed snow maiden, her hair still spinning gold out of grey, her eyes and mouth still ill-defined holes. Cold sprayed over him in specks that burned; he twitched phantasmal armor around himself.

And then the mist cleared and Trey looked out at dozens of snow maidens, intermingled with cobwebbed cloaks and small black barghests with fiery-coal eyes.

"Come on then," he said, beckoning. "Who's first?"

The wraiths fell in swathes before Sorrow. The half-formed creatures were no match for him.

If only there weren't so many of them, crowding together, reaching out with plucking fingers, snapping muzzles, and tangling folds.

Trey suspected that they were only there to slow him down.

Which meant *someone* didn't want him reaching—

A familiar shriek pierced his senses. "*Trey!*"

The mist had cleared, leaving him in the middle of a steel-grey plain with a high-vaulted ceiling of milky-white. Distant figures were pinned to it; they writhed like insects. Trey didn't spare them too close a look.

"Arabella, here!" he called back as he decapitated a barghest. Smoky flames spurted out of its severed neck, consuming both head and body. Trey put his gauntleted arm in front of his face and thrust himself through a crowd of cloaks. It was like forcing his way through layers of draperies.

Draperies that whispered and gibbered, reminding him of every sin, every nightmare.

As if he hadn't hardened himself against everything they could throw at him. *Brother-killer. Pervert. Liar.*

Trey spoke a few curt words and his armor turned white-hot and flared. Cloaks disintegrated in the blast.

"Trey!" Arabella came scrambling over the edge of the plain, tripping over her feet, clutching something to her chest. "Help me!"

And behind her, like a towering thundercloud with eyes of fire, a massive hell hound heaved itself onto the plain.

What a monster! Trey thought appreciatively, resting Sorrow on his shoulder.

The creature's muscles rippled under its coal-black hide. Its paws were as big as carriages. Strands of toxic slobber fell from its mouth, the ground smoking underneath. Its growl reverberated against the arched ceiling. The skeletal figures affixed to it stopped their struggles and held still in fear.

Arabella was pale against the hell hound's tar-black bulk, still running, still valiant.

Not that she had any hope of outdistancing it.

The hell hound stretched out its neck, mouth with double rows of teeth and black gums, wide open. It loomed over Arabella, then lowered its jaws with a snap.

On empty air.

One moment she was in the blast of its fetid breath, the next Trey jerked the life line she gripped.

Arabella stumbled upon landing and pitched forward into his chest. He caught her around the waist, steadying her.

"Sorry," she said, the word muffled.

The hell hound raised its muzzle in a howl so bone-chilling that Arabella quivered and clutched the lapels of his coat even tighter.

"Hey, now." Trey gently held her away from him, one hand on her shoulder. "Don't you have the vapors right now. You're a game one, aren't you?"

Some color returned to her pale face. Arabella caught her breath in a half-sob and half-gulp and bit her lip. She nodded.

There were tears on her face, the first Trey had seen so far in her adventure.

He left Sorrow point-down next to him, and pulled a mist-thin handkerchief from his equally insubstantial coat pocket. With calm practicality, he dabbed her face, seemingly paying no attention to the hell hound galloping towards them.

Arabella glanced nervously over her shoulder.

"Don't worry about the friend you brought," Trey told her, reaching for another one of his lines. He jerked them both to another part of the plain, and once again, the thwarted hound raised up its cry.

Arabella stared at him. "You're," she said, almost accusingly, poking his shoulder, "a *ghost*." Her finger pressed into him with a feeling that was half-ticklish, half-prickly.

"I had to leave my body behind." The hell hound's giant head appeared once more. Once again, it ran for them in ground-eating strides. "Tell me what happened, Arabella. I can only use my life lines two or three more times." Already short-lived, they were crumbling rapidly.

The usual spells and runes didn't last long in the Shadow Lands.

She nodded, face set and determined. There were smudges on her face and her skirt was sadly tattered.

She looked adorable.

Not the time to be thinking of such things,

"There was someone else in the pawnshop besides Mr. Gibbs. But he—or she—did something to my memory so I can't remember him or her at all. The same person trapped me in a pentagram using my mother's ring." She held up her right hand with a dainty gesture.

"Effective, but with a glaring weakness you obviously exploited. Excuse me, Arabella." Trey put an arm around her again and shifted them again.

She was still talking, the words tumbling out of her. "It was a trap for *you*. They meant for you to follow me. The ghoul was there, too." She shuddered.

Trey couldn't blame her.

"And," Arabella went on, triumphantly, "I remembered what was going on in the pawnshop. A miasma attack at the *Viewing* tomorrow!"

A feeling, part-fear, part-excitement, clenched in his gut. "Well done," he said softly. "And now, I think, it's time you returned to your body, Arabella." Her exertions had done her spirit no good—her feet had completely lost shape, so that she appeared to be gliding on a column of light.

"Yes, but what of *that*?" The hell hound appeared on the horizon again.

"I'll get you on your way." His last life line had, as planned, found her body. He grabbed a hold of it for their last shift.

They landed in a different place this time. Under a polished silver sky, the hard silver ground was strewn with gem stones, like pebbles on a shore. Some were cut and polished, others still rough. They glittered in a rainbow of colors. Ruined structures and worn statuary were scattered throughout.

It wasn't far enough. The hell hound had already turned even before they manifested, was already arrowing right for them.

The creature had known he would save this for last.

The creature? Or its master?

Arabella looked wildly around. "Oh!" Her stare fixed on a yellow topaz, clear in parts, smoky in others. She reached down to touch it, then sprang back, hiding her eyes, as it flared to life.

A portal stood where the stone had been, stretching into a tunnel that seemed to be made of water, walls rippling in bands of blue, green, and grey.

Arabella hurried eagerly towards it—it could hardly be helped, since the tug of her body at the other end was so strong.

But, incredibly, she checked herself at the entrance. "What about you?" she asked. "I can't leave you with that thing!"

Her misplaced concern was touching. "Have you no faith, Miss Trent?" said Trey lightly, going up to her. He dropped a kiss on her upturned forehead. "I'm the Shade Hunter. Now get going!" He gave her a little push; the portal did the rest.

Currents of color, smelling of good earth and green herbs, enveloped her. The portal vanished.

Trey swung Sorrow, the blade whistling through aether. "Come on, you hell hound! Come and fight!"

It came at him, bigger than a house, bigger than a church even.

Yes, this would be a tough battle.

One that he wouldn't have to fight.

As the hell hound galloped up, its reek of old blood and rot surging ahead of it, drool splattering and smoking, Trey felt that familiar pinch between his shoulder blades.

About time, thought Trey, as Winter and the rest finally got ahold of him and yanked him back to Vaeland.

Trey opened his eyes and sat up, his hands clenched around the sides of a thinly-padded mahogany box too much like a coffin.

This was one of the reasons he didn't much like spirit walking.

By the grey light creeping through the attic windows, he could tell it was morning. Trey looked around at the strained, exhausted faces peering at him and found Winter.

He said, before Winter could scold him for his actions regarding the anchoring spell, "There's going to be a miasma attack." Trey stood up and stepped over the side of the box. "At the Viewing."

Chapter Fourteen

JONATHAN BLAKE WAS UNEASY, a feeling that lay like lead in his gut. The soft dimness of dawn reigned inside the old Keep, the Vaelish people's first and oldest safe haven. Night's chill seeped through the stone walls of the long waiting chamber, the woolen tapestries depicting scenes from Vaeland's perilous past doing little to hold back the cold. The air was still and musty; a reverent hush filled the place. Any inadvertent sound—a scuffle, a deep breath—seemed to be amplified tenfold.

This was not the first time Blake had drawn this duty, but familiarity had not taken the edge off his wariness.

Unknown to most, *this* was the most dangerous time of the Vernal Rites, this in-between time as night gave way to day on the morning of the Viewing. The Mirror of Elsinore was already in place in the ancient solar, and the only physical entrance to that chamber was through this room.

The gilded and gaudy artifact that the city burghers paraded in the streets later that day was only a decoy for the real thing. Two Guardians had brought the Mirror from its secret home in Flurrey last night and installed it in the solar, where they waited to complete the rites of renewal.

After last year's Incursion and the long winter, the restoration of the Mirror's powers was desperately needed.

Swan, the aquamentalist, shifted next to him. This was her first big assignment, and nervous excitement and determined duty were writ all over her square face. Short and curly-headed, she seemed to disappear in the large wraith cloak she wore.

The wraith cloaks. Another thing that only increased Blake's unease. Fantastically expensive, the cloaks were woven out of phantasmia, spider silk, and the light of a half moon. He had no idea how Internal Affairs had managed to come up with six of them for the elementalists and magicians that guarded the Mirror.

They hadn't ever done so before.

Maybe this was caution after the Great Incursion last year. Or maybe they suspected an attack.

Wraith cloaks to protect against Shadow Lands demons and shades.

Blake didn't like this one bit.

He queried Ember, his fire elemental. The salamander, uncharacteristically serious, was on patrol duty, stretching thin strands of purifying fire across windows and doorways.

Should anything unclean enter the Keep, he would know it.

Swan said in a whisper, "Aria and Crescendo report no trouble, sir." She almost managed to keep her voice even.

"Good. Ask them to come back in." Blake called for Ember, and the salamander leapt from the wall to his shoulder in a flame-colored streak. Cool, sinuous bodies brushed past Blake as Swan's undines flowed from the wall and coiled up her legs. She took their watery bodies in a hand each, petting and cooing, and they curled into twin bracelets, grey and ropey, on her wrists.

A movement in the short hallway leading out of the solar caught Blake's attention. The Guardians emerged and stood in the doorway.

The sturdier of the two, a curly-headed broad-faced man who went by the name of Mr. Milton, nodded at him. From the lilt in his voice, Blake guessed he came from one of the counties that bordered Alfheim, the elven kingdom to the north. Blake had no doubt the Guardian's false name was related to his profession; the man's jacket was dusted with flour and a smell of yeast surrounded him.

Ember made a contented sound that could only be interpreted as *Mmm.* Fresh-baked buns were among her favorite foods.

After this is over, we'll get a whole bag of them to share, he told her. The salamander stroked his cheek in response, the caress a pleasant tingle.

The other Guardian was a small, fidgety man with the bright beady eyes and darting movements of a bird. He dressed like a magpie, too, with odd bits of finery here and there amongst his shabby clothes—a glittering pin holding his neckerchief in place, a swatch of butterfly-patterned silk peeking from a pocket, brass trinkets attached to chains at his waist.

He hadn't been introduced to Blake at all. Mr. Milton had done all the talking while the birdlike man stared out of large, clear gold eyes.

Mr. Milton opened his mouth.

Blake never knew what he meant to say. The warning came a fraction of a moment before the attack.

Alarms blared. A blast shook the edifice. Fires roared in the outer chambers of the Keep.

Swan started. "What?"

"Protect the Guardians and the solar!" Blake dashed towards the doorway, Ember's fire running down his arm and glowing around his hand.

He burst into an outer chamber, one that had once been a dining hall. Marius charged into the room from the other end, a bullish man with heavy brows and a habitual scowl, who was, rather surprisingly, an aeromentalist.

"Report!" Blake demanded.

"Bastards took out my whirlwinds," grunted Marius. "Banged my flock up good, too." Sylphs lay around his shoulders like gauzy scarves, uttering piteous squeaks.

"Demons?"

"No." Marius shook his head. "Men, in odd garb."

"Be ready!" Blake warned. "Here they come!"

Footsteps pounded up the stairs. Blake caught sight of a strange, bulbous head for an instant, before it disappeared with a yelp as the steps crumbled.

Bard and his stanae. The earth elementals had collapsed the stairs. Marius gave a pleased grunt.

Blake had no time to express approval. Thanks to his sympathetic connection with Ember, he could summon fire. He set curtains of it across the doorway and windows. Marius didn't need to be asked—his flock launched and fanned the flames ever higher.

The fire crackled hungrily, burning without fuel. Blake slid a vial of salt from his belt and tossed its contents into the flames. They spat furiously. Twisted spires of green and blue danced within them.

Impfire, malicious and painful, ready to inflict stinging burns on any who dared pass through.

Blake put his hand on a vial of gold flakes in aqua sancta. Expensive, hard to get, hard to make, this would burn away all impure thoughts—frequently along with the person harboring them, too.

No, they'd need a prisoner or two to interrogate.

Marius' flock pushed the flames down the stairs.

Both men waited, tense.

And then came the surge.

A wave of thick black smoke spilled out from the stairwell. The flames whipped and danced; Blake poured more power into them. Smoke and fire fought, coiling around each other like aggressive snakes. The sylphs, now visible as myriad translucent and winged creatures, also formed into currents, pushing back the onslaught.

Fire and air lost.

Smoke rushed into the chamber, filling it up in moments. The fire extinguished immediately and fragile air elementals died in scores. Marius howled outrage, the sound quickly choked off.

The stench of grave dirt told Blake all he needed to know.

This wasn't smoke.

It was miasma.

"Fall back, man," he gasped out, pulling the hood over his face and drawing the cloak tighter around himself. Ember hissed and clung to his shoulder, pressed against his neck. Miasma brushed Blake's hand, sending searing pain up his arm. He jerked his hand back into his sleeve.

"Don't let it touch—" he yelled.

Marius screamed.

And kept on screaming.

Great Saints! Blake staggered through the miasma towards the aeromentalist. He didn't dare look up, for fear the stuff would get in his eyes. All he could see in his truncated vision was roiling black smoke, dry in his nose, ashy against his lips, stinging against his face.

He banged painfully into something, nearly falling over it. Just in time he kept himself from stretching out his hands for support.

Miasma rolled up against Blake's legs, turning the hem of his cloak black and shriveled. Blake stumbled around, yelling for Marius to put up his hood and tuck in his cloak. He cursed as he stumbled over chairs and footstools, one of which completely disintegrated into a foul-smelling ash.

Not good!

Marius' scream dropped to a raw whisper, then a gurgle.

And then it stopped.

Blake stood, panting, sweating, ears strained. "Marius?"

No reply. He closed his eyes, stomach churning at the thought of what the miasma had done to the man.

And what it was going to do to *him*. The hem of the cloak had frayed and he was completely turned around in this chamber. Where was the doorway? Ember hummed her distress as fear spurted through him.

It's all right, pet, he soothed, knowing how futile and empty the comfort was.

He had the sense of the room growing larger around him, becoming cavernous, filling up with darkness. The floor stretched for miles around him, and Blake stood rooted to the spot, unable to pick a direction.

He'd stand here until the miasma nibbled the wraith cloak to shreds, then did the same thing to his flesh. Panic swelled inside him; Blake clenched his hands hard, digging his fingernails into his palms. The small pain helped stemmed the tide of emotion somewhat, giving him time to gather his composure.

The room didn't grow. It's the miasma playing with my mind.

Blake focused on his breathing, his bond with Ember. Without the rasp of his panic in his ears and the drumbeat of his heart pounding against his ribs, he could push through the miasma's illusion. The room wavered, two perceptions fighting each other.

Help, God-Father.

And then he heard it—the sound of a flute, sweet and high and piercing. It brought with it coolness and space and... rain?

It was raining in the chamber. Ropes of water fell, splattering and splashing the unseen floor. Miasma gave way before it, falling into a sludge, clearing the chamber. Blake blinked; he could see the walls and windows again, a glimpse of the scarred and blackened oak table.

A charred hulk on the floor that could only be Marius.

His gorge rose. Blake pressed his lips together tightly and turned back towards the waiting room. A waterfall covered the doorway, gushing ferociously, spraying back up from the floor in a mist. The undines churned through it as the flute played, fast, urgent, calling him.

Blake plunged through the water barrier. Instantly drenched to the skin, he emerged on the other side with all his clothes sticking to him. The incredibly costly wraith cloak was in rags hanging from his shoulders.

Swan stood in the middle of the waiting chamber, flute to her lips, her face sheened with sweat, her eyes wide with fear. The two Guardians hovered in the hallway to the solar, the bird man running his chains through his hands and muttering, Mr. Milton shaping and patting something invisible.

"Keep going, Swan," Blake told her hoarsely. He could feel the spell taking shape as the Guardians wove it to protect the Mirror.

Protecting *them*, though? That was his and Swan's job.

Get to it, Ember.

The salamander darted out, a ball of anger and determination, mirroring his own emotions. She shot in lines in front of the rippling waterfall, leaving scorch marks on stone and fiery ropes in the air.

Swan's arms trembled; she couldn't hold on much longer.

Blake uncapped the vial of gold flakes and threw the contents onto the barrier Ember had erected. The whole thing flared up into a wall of gold and red, floor to ceiling.

Swan's hands dropped, the flute crashing to the floor. She doubled over, arms at her side, panting as if she'd run a mile.

Her undines stroked across the floor and clung to her legs in twin folds. Their fear was palpable.

Yet they'd held the line, as had Swan.

She deserves a commendation. Blake thought, as he raised his hands and fed more power to his barrier. There were three layers to it, and he tossed another vial, this one of silver flakes in lily-and-moonlight-steeped water.

Whitish flames rose between him and the gold ones. The last shield.

Swan straightened, still gasping. "What else can I do, sir?"

"Pray," said Blake, intent on the fire.

What had happened to the other elementalists downstairs? Dead, most likely. But someone had to have noticed the miasma. The alarms had to be going off all over the Quadrangle.

"Help's on the way," he said out loud, for Swan's benefit.

It had to be.

Because not even gold flames could hold back the miasma.

Beyond the fiery wall, something thudded and rolled, chinking like glass, heavy like a cannonball.

And then it exploded.

Miasma broke through the barriers an instant before Blake grabbed Swan's arm and thrust her into the wall at the far side. He grabbed the edge of her hood and pulled it over her face.

"Keep covered!" he ordered, spinning around, flames in his hands.

Two men entered along with the miasma, wearing black oval masks with blank eyes of colored glass. Dressed in tight black, their masks looked too heavy for their necks.

One of them stooped and rolled a black glass ball towards the Guardians, still working their spell to protect the Mirror.

Not on my... Blake launched himself at it, knowing he would be too late.

The sphere burst open.

Trey sped along the boundary of the Shadow Lands, the mortal realm bunching and stretching on one side of him. Images flashed by, too fast to register more than impressions: a chamber maid with dirty bare feet making up a fire; a man carefully shaving in front of a small mirror; a stable boy curled in the straw with two sleeping hounds.

Tendrils of black vapor wafted towards him in a whiff of acid. The Keep rose up ahead of him, seen as though under water, stained with black ink.

Miasma. They had attacked, then.

Trey's mouth set in a hard line. The air around him turned thick as he slowed. He teased phantasmia through his fingers, subduing it, winding it into a ball, working quickly. It was far better to prepare the stuff beforehand, rather than pull it raw from the Shadow Lands.

In an emergency, he'd rather have phantasmia. He'd gladly answer for it later, when everyone was safe.

Trey waited, though every instinct screamed at him to run in.

The others needed time, and miasma was nasty stuff even to a phantasmist.

Trey's senses prickled. Denizens of the Shadow Lands had taken notice of the incident. They watched from a distance, waiting for an opening. None of them was a big threat on its own.

For now, Trey could ignore them.

Silver runes twinkled to life around the Keep, their gleam distorted and tarnished through the ever-moving boundary. Winter.

It was time.

He moved through sludge. One more step and he was both still in the Shadow Lands and inside the Keep.

He saw the attackers in their protective armor, saw the miasma sphere roll across the room. Saw Blake move—*heroic idiot!* —to throw himself on top of it in a futile, desperate gesture.

Trey cut a long rip with Sorrow and stepped into the room.

Miasma roiled up into his face. He grimaced, catching it between phantasmia-gloved hands. The stuff writhed, fighting him, as he encased it in phantasmia. Splinters of emotion—anger, jealousy, fear—pricked him; Trey solidified his mental defenses against them.

These weapons were of a crude, brute-force type. They'd been made by men, not demons.

Once the phantasmia had taken hold, he whisked both substances back into the Shadow Lands.

One of the masked men uttered an inarticulate yell and tossed another globe in Trey's direction. It crashed to the floor in a shower of glass shards.

Trey lunged with Sorrow, the sword an extension of his arm. The blade bit into the packed miasma, her power joining with Trey's. The sensation was cool and familiar, tinged with regret, strengthened by duty.

The miasma stuck to the blade. Black thoughts crawled into his head: *he never loved you... she should've been yours... what do these fools know?*

Sorrow pulsed, and the miasma turned to vapor and vanished. Without missing a note, Trey made a number of small cuts in the air.

Narrow slits shimmered in the air around the room, drawing in the remaining miasma. It resisted; Trey made a sharp gesture, and the miasma was sucked back into the demonic realms it had come from.

The masked men turned and fled. Trey pinched the boundary between his fingers, slid into the Shadow Lands, and reappeared at the door, his wraith sword pointed at one's neck.

"Stay where you are, gentlemen," he said pleasantly. "I'll have a few questions for you, momentarily." He looked over their shoulders and flashed a grin at Blake still crouched on the floor. "Old fellow, you look rather worse for the wear."

Blake rose shakily to his feet. Ember, pale and dim, clung to his shoulder. "About time you got here," he muttered. "Sorry for taking you away from an assembly."

Trey realized that he was still in tail coat and knee-breeches. "Never mind about that," he said, as the other phantasmists ran into the chamber. First among them was Winter, runes flashing like blades all around him.

"Now, then," said Trey softly, his attention back on the masked men. "Which one of you will talk first?"

"Twelve Saints!" Atwater halted at the top of the stairs into the outer chamber. The miasma was gone and the burned remains of the aeromentalist removed, but the wrecked furniture and acrid odor remained.

Atwater's gaze was riveted to the scarred table top, upon which lay glass-eyed masks, leather pouches, and yards of wraith cloth. Spheres of black glass lay next to the pile. Atwater gave them a hard, suspicious stare.

Trey kept a bland expression on his own face. They'd disposed of the miasma within the globes, but Atwater didn't need to know that yet.

"Have a seat, Reginald." Winter indicated one of the great chairs pulled up to the table. They'd had to fetch it from another room. "I'm glad you could come. My apologies for calling you away from home so early this morning."

Trey had to admire his supervisor's composure. Winter betrayed no hint of his knowledge of Atwater's clandestine meeting last night. Sutton had traced Trey's spell on the man to a wharfside tavern whose keeper confessed to having rented out an outbuilding to a bunch of seedy characters. Morgan and Jem's investigation of the place confirmed traces of miasma: eaten-away furniture, broken glass, and one shriveled, unidentifiable corpse.

Miasma was dangerous, as these plotters had discovered. Maybe the lesson would stick.

"We need to ensure the populace isn't thrown into a panic over this incident," Winter continued, tone measured.

Atwater relaxed a little. "Indeed," he said smoothly, seating himself in a way that could only be described as regal. As a Member of Parliament he officially outranked the government functionaries in the room, never mind that Trey was a Viscount and Winter a Master in the Magisterium. "The damage could've been worse. I commend you gentlemen on your quick response."

"Not quick enough," said Trey. "An aeromentalist died in this very room." A geomentalist and two other magicians had also perished below. He'd known none of them, but Blake had. Remembering the look on his friend's face, he was coldly angry.

Atwater glanced at the pocked and blackened stones where Marius had met his unpleasant demise. "Most unfortunate."

"And not something we need to spread abroad," Winter broke in with a quelling frown at Trey. "As far as the public needs to know, the Mirror won't arrive at the Keep until the Procession in about an hour."

"Agreed," said Atwater.

"What I don't know is how the attackers learned the Mirror was already here." Winter folded his arms.

Atwater shrugged. "I'm afraid in certain quarters it is more or less common knowledge. Far too many people know of the deception, and anyone paying close attention to the movements of known government magicians would soon put the pieces together. In your zeal to provide protection, August, you could've inadvertently shown your hand."

Trey longed to punch the man's smug face. Didn't the windbag find his own posturing tiring?

"That is something to be careful of in the future." Winter took this criticism with equanimity.

Atwater eyed the masks again. "What happened to the perpetrators?" he asked with a forced casualness.

"We detained them," said Winter blandly. Atwater stiffened. Winter went on, "But, unfortunately, someone had planted a nasty death spell on them. They both died shortly after."

Atwater made some commiserating noises that struck Trey as completely false, and rose to his feet. "If there's nothing else to talk about, Winter, I'd best be off to reassure the prime minister and the Prince Regent before the Procession." He rose to his feet.

Trey said, before he could take his leave, "You'll be happy to know the young lady who suffered the accident from the runaway carriage will recover shortly."

"Indeed, I'm happy to hear of Miss Trent's recovery. Please convey my—" Atwater stopped as Winter's eyes narrowed.

"Miss Trent?" said Winter in a soft voice so filled with ice and steel that Trey wasn't surprised to see Atwater falter. "How come you to know the young lady's name, Reginald?"

For a moment, naked terror was plain on Atwater's face. Then he gave a little laugh. "Ah, I must've heard it somewhere, seen it in the papers, or something,"

"You couldn't have," Winter went on in that same cold voice. "I made sure to leave the young lady's name out of any written communication. Only her family and a select few of her friends even knew of her accident, and the only ones to connect her to the pawnshop were me, Shield… and now you."

Atwater paled and flushed by turns. "What are you saying, August? Surely you aren't accusing me of—" His hands clenched and Trey's hands twitched for Sorrow. Let the man make even one threatening move—

Winter gave his friend a look devoid of pity—or any other emotion. "Why did you do it, Reggie? You, of all people?"

All the fight went out of the other man. He sank into his chair, deflating like a punctured balloon, and put his head into his hands.

"It wasn't supposed to go this far," he said, voice muffled. "I only meant to shake things up a bit, scare people, turn them against Internal Affairs."

Winter's eyebrows shot up. "Turn them against Internal Affairs?" he repeated. "You, who have been a staunch supporter your entire political career? In the name of the Twelve Saints, *why?*"

Atwater lifted a face old and lined and bitter. "And much good it's done me! There's no money in it, is there? All the new financiers, industrialists, and mercantile companies are agitating to relax the regulations the government imposes on magic use…"

"Like, perhaps, bringing miasma from the Shadow Lands?" interrupted Trey. He glared at Atwater, who wouldn't meet his eyes.

Or Winter's.

"Which groups financed you?" demanded Winter, leaning forward, his knuckles white on the chair back. "Who supplied you with the miasma?"

Atwater pressed his lips together and shook his head. A crafty look had come into his eyes. "I won't say any more. This is not a trial; I'm not required to speak."

"Don't make this worse for yourself, Reggie," Winter warned.

"Oh, it can't get much worse than it already is," Atwater answered. "But I won't just give myself to the hangman's noose. You want names, you're going to have to pay for them."

They stared at each other, Winter pale and contemptuous, Atwater flushed and belligerent.

"Very well," said Winter, "if that's the game you want to play. But you will understandably be detained." He nodded to the Home Office constables waiting against the wall. They came forward with magic-sealing manacles.

Atwater held out his wrists with no further complaints. His eyes were on Winter as they yanked him to this feet. "Well, you did advise me to give up politics, August."

And with a bitter chuckle, he let himself be led away.

Arabella Trent opened her eyes and stared up at a familiar ceiling covered in painted pink roses and yellow tulips.

She felt oddly heavy. Weights seemed to be attached to her lids, so that it took great effort to keep them open. Her eyes felt gummy, her head weighed as much as a cannonball, and as for the rest of her…

And then she remembered.

Arabella gasped and jumped up.

Or at least, she tried to. But what emerged from her stiff lips was a low moan, and all her body did was twitch a bit.

Her body, that she now inhabited.

Arabella's hands were still crossed on her chest. Her fingers tightened around each other, seeking her ring. The sapphire pressed into her hand, and a small smile curved her dry lips.

Hurrah, she thought, too tired to do much more. After being lighter than air, she'd have to get used to her corporeal form again.

She lay for a few minutes, reveling in the sound and feel of her body. The rhythm of her own breathing, the pounding of her heart, the gurgle of her insides…

Oh. She was hungry.

Arabella levered herself up onto an elbow and eased herself up the pillows. The movement took far longer than it should've, and she was panting with exhaustion after.

Clearly, she needed nourishment.

Arabella lay back against the pillows for a while, then reached out for the bell pull. Her hand was loose around it, but she managed to tug it down. Once, twice, thrice.

She didn't have long to wait. Voices called and footsteps sounded, the door crashed open, and suddenly the room was full of people.

Aunt Cecilia, still in her night dress and wrapper, just kept herself from throwing herself at Arabella, instead clinging to her hand, saying over and over again, "He was right! He was right! Just leave her be to come back to herself, he said. He was right!"

The maids crying and dabbing their eyes behind her. A ghastly-looking Harry leaning against the doorjamb in weak-kneed relief; Uncle Henry misty-eyed and polishing his spectacles furiously next to him.

"Well," he said, frowning at his work and blinking rapidly. "Well, well."

Arabella looked at them all, loving them, smiling so hard it was a wonder her face didn't crack. "Well," she said, her voice cracking instead. "I'm back."

Chapter Fifteen

Several days later, Arabella alighted from a hackney, too impatient to let Jonathan Blake open the door for her.

"Be careful, Arabella," Charlotte called after her. "Remember, you're still recovering!"

Arabella swung around and turned a laughing face up at Charlotte's anxious one. "I am miles better," she declared. "I could've walked here perfectly easily, I'm sure."

"I'm glad you didn't try," said Charlotte tartly, as her brother helped her out. It was hard to tell who was supporting whom, since Blake had also been injured on the day of the Viewing. "I'd have hated to have you fainting halfway here. What a bore that would be!"

That was more like the Charlotte she knew. Arabella wasn't used to the other girl being solicitous.

The air was mild, the sunshine young that morning. The characteristic soot and sewage smell of the City had retreated. Arabella looked around at the brick townhouses and iron lamps, marveling at how commonplace and unthreatening they looked.

It was hard to believe she'd taken an unnerving walk through these streets as a ghost, the Shadow Lands cold against her back.

Arabella shook out the folds of her pelisse and tried not to skip with impatience. "Are you sure he'll be there?" she queried Blake.

The young man flashed her a smile. He was still pale and quiet, but his expression was warm enough. "Aye. I had Sutton send me a message when he left the Quadrangle."

Blake turned to the hackney driver, telling him to wait for them. Arabella patted the placid horse, relishing how the creature didn't do anything more alarming than swish its tail.

Then she looked at the houses ahead eagerly. A familiar figure sprang up the stoop of one. Even if she hadn't recognized his face, she'd have known that sense of coiled energy right away.

"Lord St. Ash," she called out, heedless of the stares of passersby—of which there were only two: a servant out with a shopping basket and a wiry chimney sweep with his long-handled brush on his shoulder and his flock of soot-filled sylphs bunched up behind him.

For a moment, she had the hideous conviction Trey would ignore her—as would be well within his rights. Properly brought up young ladies didn't call out to their gentlemen acquaintances from down the street.

But then he stopped and turned, and Arabella's diminished happiness bubbled up yet again.

Really, it was wonderful to be alive and no amount of rudeness or snubbing should affect her good temper.

She hurried over to the steps of his residence and stood smiling up at him. It was past Holy Week, and she had recovered considerably. The bruise on her cheek, its healing aided by an herbalist's potion, was faint enough to be hidden under a thin layer of powder.

Trey looked rather stiff and somewhat tired and preoccupied. But as Arabella beamed at him, his lips twitched in answer. "Haven't you learned not to go traipsing into undesirable neighborhoods yet, Miss Trent?"

Arabella tilted her head towards the Blake siblings, hanging further back. Charlotte was fussing over her long-suffering brother and pointedly not looking at them. "I brought companions this time."

Trey looked over her shoulder at Blake. "Traitor," he muttered.

Arabella didn't think that warranted the dignity of a response. Instead she said, "You've been avoiding me." She tilted her head. "I sent you a letter."

"I read it," he answered.

It had taken her most of a morning to compose the missive, necessitating the use of several sheets of paper before she'd been happy with the result. "But you didn't reply," she pointed out.

"I'm embarrassed by gratitude."

"I'm afraid I shall have to embarrass you further." Arabella held out a paper-wrapped package. "This is to thank you for all your help. I am greatly in your debt."

"Miss Trent, you did as much to save yourself—and helped protect the Mirror into the bargain." He took the package, handling it so gingerly and with such patent misgiving that Arabella bit her lip to keep from laughing.

"They're only cakes," she told him. "For your sadly reduced larder." Her voice held a teasing note, but Trey Shield was having none of it.

"Thank you." He bowed. "Your servant, Miss Trent." Once more, he turned to the door.

What would it take to get a smile or an amused gleam from him? Apparently, he was only at ease around the disembodied.

"Wait," she said sharply. Lowering her voice, she added, "What of the ghoul?"

The tensing of his shoulders told her the answer. "I regret it has eluded for now. But that is no longer your concern. If you'll excuse me." And with that, he entered his house and shut the door behind him with a decisive click.

Arabella stared at the faded paint on the door, a frown between her eyes. That the ghoul was still at large was worrisome.

The Blake siblings came up to her. "Rude as ever," commented Charlotte, followed by her brother's resigned, "I told you he'd be like that."

Arabella nodded. It was hard to think that a few days ago, Trey Shield had dropped a kiss on her forehead in the Shadow Lands.

Or maybe she'd just imagined the whole thing. There were several exciting things going on at the time, after all.

Then she chuckled softly. Blake turned an inquiring look at her.

"At least," said Arabella, with a mischievous grin, "he took the cakes."

As Charlotte linked arms with her, she cast another look at the Shade Hunter's dwelling. They would see each other socially. He could hardly ignore her on every single occasion.

Besides, she had questions. Many of them.

Another time, she promised herself—and him. *There'll be another time.*

Epilogue

LORD ATWATER SAT IN A DIM dank cell in Harrowgate prison, a tight smile on his lips.

He would sell his secrets dearly. For days, he'd stalled all the questioners and interrogators. No one had cast spells on him, for magically-obtained testimony was inadmissible in court. No one had brought out a medieval rack or thumbscrews. Everyone had chided and remonstrated and appealed to his higher nature.

Lord Atwater had long since wrestled with his higher nature, defeated it, and buried it deep. Appeals to it meant nothing to him now.

All he waited for was how much the other side would pay to buy his silence.

And finally, they came.

There was a shift in the darkness, a ripple in the air. Lord Atwater lifted his head and said, low, but impatiently, "You finally made contact. Weren't you afraid—?"

There was a taste of cold ice and sweet rot on his lips. The air around him chilled instantly.

Atwater's eyes rounded. "No!" he breathed to the newcomer. "No, you don't understand—!"

The ghoul lunged.

Much later, the ghoul oozed into a ramshackle building that had once housed a gaming hell and brothel. The damp from the river had gotten into everything. The wood was wet and warped, the paper moldy and peeling, the titillating murals on the ceiling faded and stained.

Old passions still lingered in the long-abandoned place—hatred, bitterness, rage, lust, all kinds of twisted appetites. To the ghoul, they tasted sweet, almost slaking his desire for the delicious soul that had slipped past him days ago.

The Master sat on a reclining sofa, eating pickled plums. "Well?"

"It is done," hissed the ghoul.

"And the Mirror?"

The ghoul laughed, without sound. "They have no suspicion that the miasma attack was only a distraction."

"Indeed," said the Master. "As planned."

"But it is such a small speck of corruption, such a minute stain. Will it be enough by the time we're ready to move?"

"Oh, yes." The Master inspected a plum, popped it into his mouth. "It will be enough."

About the Author

I create weird worlds full of magic and machines and write characters struggling to do what's right. I'm fascinated by light and darkness, transformation, and things that fly. Giant squid and space dragons appear in my work—you have been warned!

A native of Pakistan, I now reside in Northern Virginia, where I read, write, doodle, avoid housework, and homeschool my children.

Visit me online at http://www.rabiagale.com. I love hearing from readers!

Books by Rabia Gale

The Reflected City

The Shadow Lands hunger for mortal passions and human souls. A lord and a debutante stand in their way.

Ghostlight

Coming Soon: **Ghoulfire**

The Sunless World

To save their world, the mages of old plunged it into eternal darkness. It's time to bring back the light.

Quartz

Flare

Flux

Taurin's Chosen

A failed hero who has lost his faith. A woman turned demon, held together by hers. Their encounter leads to a second chance for them both.

Mourning Cloak

Ironhand

Rainbird

A half-breed in hiding. A world lit by a dragon's eye. And the sabotage that threatens them both.

Rainbird

Made in the USA
San Bernardino, CA
08 November 2018